THE ENCHANTED ISLE

Further Titles by Cynthia Harrod-Eagles

To follow from Severn House in this series:

EVEN CHANCE
LAST RUN
ON WINGS OF LOVE
RAINBOW SUMMER
ROMANY MAGIC
TITLE ROLE
THE UNFINISHED
A WELL PAINTED PASSION

The Dynasty Series:

THE FOUNDING
THE DARK ROSE
THE PRINCELING
THE OAK APPLE
THE BLACK PEARL
THE LONG SHADOW
THE CHEVALIER
THE MAIDEN
THE FLOOD-TIDE
THE TANGLED THREAD
THE EMPEROR
THE VICTORY
THE REGENCY
THE CAMPAIGNERS
THE RECKONING
THE DEVIL'S HORSE
THE POISON TREE

The Kirov Trilogy:

ANNA
FLEUR
EMILY

Detective Novels:

ORCHESTRATED DEATH
DEATH WATCH
NECROCHIP

THE ENCHANTED ISLE

Cynthia Harrod-Eagles

466712

This first world edition published in Great Britain 1993 by
SEVERN HOUSE PUBLISHERS LTD of
9–15 High Street, Sutton, Surrey SM1 1DF.
First published in the U.S.A. 1994 by
SEVERN HOUSE PUBLISHERS INC., of
475 Fifth Avenue, New York, NY 10017.

British Library Cataloguing in Publication Data
Harrod-Eagles, Cynthia
   Enchanted Isle
   I. Title
   823.914 [F]

   ISBN 0-7278-4568-3

Typeset by Hewer Text Composition Services, Edinburgh.
Printed and bound in Great Britain by
Redwood Books Trowbridge, Wiltshire.

CHAPTER ONE

It was blazing hot when the aircraft finally curved its flight in over Athens at the end of a three-and-a-half hour journey from London. Sarah Foster felt quite sick with it, and not at all as if she was starting her holiday. She hated flying – she had not done it often enough to regard it as a boring necessity, and since she still expected somehow to enjoy it, it was doubly unpleasant. The tourist-class accommodation was cramped and stuffy, the food abominable, the hostesses unobliging, and to crown it all she had found herself sitting behind a chain-smoker who blew smoke back into her face the whole of the time.

The 'plane had been delayed before take-off, so they had had to sit in it on the runway for nearly half-an-hour, which added to their discomfort. Now as she peered down through the tiny porthole at the fabulous blue of the Aegean she waited for her spirits to lift, but could feel only her rising stomach.

"I think I'm going to be sick," she said.

"You're not," Greig said firmly, but without even looking up. He had been engrossed in his book since they boarded the aeroplane at Heathrow, and even now when they had their seat-belts fastened for the descent,

1

and everyone else in the 'plane was craning his neck madly to try to see the historic city below them, Greig merely turned another page and read on, making tiny, meticulous notes in the margin in pencil.

"Well if I'm not, it's no thanks to this 'plane," she said.

"Charter flights are never as comfortable as the regular runs. That's why they're cheaper," Greig said, maddeningly reasonable and even more maddeningly able to answer her without pausing in his reading.

"Can't you put that book away for a while?" she asked him, exasperated. "I don't see why you have to bring it with you anyway. What is it? *Law of Contract*," she read, peering under the cover. "It's supposed to be a holiday, you know."

"I have to do as much as I can, even on holiday – don't forget I have to face exams when I get back," he said.

"I don't see why you couldn't have taken your holidays after the exams in that case," Sarah complained.

"Because the senior members of staff get the first choice of holidays and everyone else has to fit in where they can," Greig said, abandoning his book at last to regard her with his level grey eyes.

"Well then, hurry up and get to be senior staff!"

"I can't be senior staff until I've passed these exams – and I won't pass them if I don't do enough work," Greig said. Sarah sighed. There was no getting past his logic.

"All right. I'm sorry," she said in a small voice.

"I read on the journey because there's nothing to see in a 'plane," Greig went on. "Almost everyone reads in 'planes."

2

"All right," Sarah said irritably.

"I shall have to do some work while we're on holiday too," he said. "I must do a little bit each day to keep up to date – far better that way than leave it for a fortnight and have to mug up like mad when I get back."

"All right," Sarah said again, but resignedly this time. Greig reached over and took her hand.

"I'm sorry, darling," he said, smiling down at her sympathetically. "I know it's an awful bore for you, but you know how important it is for me to do well in these exams. Competition's very fierce nowadays, and without a good pass I won't get anywhere. You want me to get a good job, don't you?"

"Yes, of course," Sarah said, feeling a little ashamed. "I do know – of course I do. You work terribly hard, and I thought you ought to take a break, that's all."

"I will," he promised, "but I can't break off completely, that's the thing."

He continued to hold her hand as the 'plane banked, losing height, and came in at last to the long tarmac strip. Her hand was embellished with the solitaire diamond ring in the platinum setting which she had worn for three years now, her engagement ring and, she sometimes thought, the only ring she would ever wear. The ring, in its way, was typical of Greig, not at all typical of Sarah. He always wanted the best, would not settle for less, and went all out for what he wanted, even if it took years to achieve.

Sarah was one of the things; his career was another. He was training to be an accountant, and he wanted to be the best accountant there was. Not for him the short-cuts: he was to be a Chartered Accountant or nothing, even though it meant five years in articles, and therefore five years before he could marry Sarah. He would not marry her until he felt he could support her in the fashion to which he would like her to be accustomed, and that meant not until he had finished his articles and got himself a proper job. And that meant not for another year at least.

Sarah was not like that at all. A happy-go-lucky kind of person, impulsive and not much given to planning anything, least of all her life, she would have married him when he first asked her and have lived with him in a tent if need be. Money enough would have been found; somewhere to live in good time; they would have got along somehow. That was her philosophy, but it would not do for Greig. He was as particular and orderly-minded as she was untidy and rash. Sometimes she wondered how it was they had ever been attracted to each other.

They had met at a party given by a mutual friend. Greig was at that time just starting his articles, and Sarah was working, as she still was, for the Department of Health and Social Security, as a clerk in the sickness benefits section. She did not particularly like her job, but then she didn't particularly dislike it either. To her work was just something you did to make enough money to live. If you could find a reasonably well-paid job that was convenient to your home and where nobody bothered you too much, that was all you could hope for. If the people you worked with were good fun too, that was a bonus.

Greig's all-absorbing interest in his career fascinated her. She had heard and read about people with careers, of course, but had never associated it with reality, for most of the people she knew felt much the same about work as

4

she did. To Greig work was the most important thing in his life, and his plans stretched ahead into an orderly and forseeable future. Sarah had difficulty in planning as far ahead as Christmas.

He was to Sarah like some fabulous person from a fairy-tale, and she had been so fascinated by him at that party that she had agreed without hesitation to meet him for a drink the following week. What he had seen in her she could not imagine, but she supposed it was the same kind of attraction of opposites. She felt that she did have some qualities that he lacked, though she would have been hard put to actually put a name to them. Greig's qualities, on the other hand, were obvious, and of the type that endeared him immediately to her parents. He was smart, intelligent, ambitious, honest, reliable, well-mannered, and careful of Sarah's welfare. Mr. and Mrs. Foster had had no hesitation when he asked them, formally, for Sarah's hand. He was exactly the kind of person they would have chosen for a son-in-law.

They told Sarah that she was very lucky.

"I know that," she had said, for she valued him for much the same qualities that they did. "But he's lucky too, you know."

"Of course, dear," they said, but not with any great conviction. They regarded Sarah as a scatterbrain, and hoped that Greig might be a good influence on her.

"It's not your fault you're perfect, of course," she had said to Greig once, "but it can be rather annoying. Try to develop some nice, normal faults, will you. Nothing too serious – just something ordinary and human."

Because it was rather offputting always to be regarded

as the lucky one, to have people express surprise that she had 'caught' Greig. Of course she was no superwoman, but she had her points – and Greig could be perfectly infuriating sometimes. It would be nice, now and then, to be appreciated.

So now, three years later, the situation was still much the same, except that Sarah had become resigned to their long engagement, and had almost ceased to look forward to the time when it would end in marriage. Marriage had become a kind of fantasy to her, on the same level as winning the pools or meeting Robert Redford – nice, but unlikely. Greig continued to be Greig, and everyone, especially her parents, continued to think her the lucky one. It was a mark of the regard in which they held him that her parents did not even raise an eyebrow at the thought of Sarah and Greig going on holiday together. They would as soon have doubted the Pope as Greig.

They were almost the last off the 'plane, for Greig would not join the throng pressing towards the door as soon as the 'plane stopped taxi-ing. He insisted that they kept their seats until the crush died down.

"It won't get us anywhere," he reasoned with her. "We'd still have to wait for our luggage, so we might as well sit here in comfort as stand in a queue."

"Comfort!" Sarah cried, frustrated.

"I'd rather sit than stand," Greig said, going back to his book.

"Oh – you!" she fumed. "Can't you see I'm excited? I've never been to Greece before. I've never been outside Europe at all. I can't wait to see it all!"

6

"You'll have to wait," he said calmly. "And Greece isn't outside Europe."

For a moment she considered flipping his book closed to annoy him, but even while she debated the idea something caught her eye – it was a face, peering through the gap between the back of her seat and the back of Greig's. The person sitting behind them was eavesdropping and finding them very amusing, by the look of him, for all she could see was a face red with suppressed mirth, and a merry eye.

Sarah turned fully to face him, ready to be indignant, but at that moment the young man stood up and fixed her with a cheerful grin to which she couldn't take exception. His expression seemed to say to her – infuriating, isn't it? What he did actually say was,

"Glad to see someone else is sensible enough not to join the crush. They only have to queue up for their luggage, so it gets them nowhere."

Greig glanced up, grunted, and glanced down again, probably without even taking in what had been said, and with the ghost of a wink at Sarah, the young man pulled down his mac from the overhead rack and sauntered out. For the life of her, she couldn't decide if he was taking the mickey or not.

At last Greig consented to move, and after a short walk across the grilling tarmac they reached the terminal to claim their luggage. Greig at last put his book away, at least for long enough to find their party. A mini-bus was laid on to take them to the dock for the small boat which would transport them to the island where they would be staying. They were the last on the bus, and Sarah felt that everyone was glaring at them for being last. She could hardly blame them – it was no fun sitting in a bus in that heat.

The journey was short, however, and being last on had its advantage, for they were first off, and were able to choose their seats on the small boat that was tied up at the bottom of the harbour steps.

"I'm glad the sea looks calm, anyway," Sarah remarked to Greig as they climbed over the gunwale. "I wouldn't like to risk a rough ride in this old tub." It was a small open boat with a tiny wheelhouse which would just house one man. There were seats right round, and a locker in the middle of the deck on which were piled boxes of groceries and other shopping. The boat had once been white, but she was now streaky yellow where the rust had soaked through her paint, and her name, painted in black across her bows and in white on the life-belt, was *Ariadne*.

"So, you like my beautiful boat?" a voice boomed in Sarah's ear, and jumping like a startled deer she turned, and saw an immensely fat, brown man grinning at her with a veritable Fort Knox of gold teeth. He was dressed in trousers cut off raggedly at the knee, and a faded shirt which parted, buttonless, at the front to show his hairy belly. On his head he wore a soiled and greasy yachting cap, by which she took him to be the captain. She blushed, wondering if he had heard what she had said, and gave him a sickly smile.

"Oh yes," she said, "it's beautiful." Cross your fingers, she told herself, to eradicate the lie.

"Yes, yes, she is beautiful, my *Ariadne*," he bellowed

back, rolling his 'r's splendidly. "A thousand thousand times she had made this journey, so that now she can find her way alone – I no longer have to steer her. Ha!" He shouted with laughter at his own joke, and Sarah smiled stickily and headed for her chosen seat in the bow.

"You don't want to sit there, you know," Greig warned her. "You'll get soaked once we're under way."

Sarah opened her mouth to argue, when she was again deafened by the large man.

"Hey, Missy! You don't want to sit there – you'll gets drowned. You come over here by Jorkos – I tell you everything you see on the way."

Sarah looked at Greig and they exchanged a shrug, and then went back to sit beside the wheelhouse where they were told. The next person on board was the insolent young man from the aeroplane, and he gave Sarah a derisive grin as he passed her and went to sit in the bow in the place Sarah had just vacated. No doubt he thought she had been moved back by Greig – at least, that's what his expression seemed to say.

It was impossible to be bad tempered now, though, now that they were out in the open air, riding gently up and down on the glassy swell of the bluest sea she had ever seen; it was bluer even than the most dishonest picture postcard. The air smelled marvellous, as if every breath was a tonic, and the fat man who had called himself Jorkos was being very friendly.

"You staying at the English Villa, on the Island? Ah, yes, you will have good time there. Mister Geralds, he owns it, makes everyone welcome like his own brothers, and the island is beautiful, beautiful – the most beautiful of all the islands. I was born there, I live there, and so I know." He rolled his eyes to emphasise his point, and looked at Sarah so meltingly that she half expected his eyes to pour down his cheeks like two black tears.

"Is the swimming nice?" she asked politely. She was a confirmed water-baby, though Greig could take it or leave it. Jorkos stared at her in disbelief.

"Swimming?" he shouted. *"Swimming?"* Sarah nodded doubtfully, wondering what she had said. "You come to my island and you ask about swimming? Madam, until you have swim in the waters of my island, you have not swim – no, no, I tell you – you have not swim ever in your life. It is the most beautiful – " He paused, and finally decided he had no words strong enough to tell her of the experience in store for her. He rolled his eyes again, and shrugged. "You see," he promised.

The boat was now full, and the luggage was all on board, and Jorkos turned away and began to be very efficient, talking in what Sarah assumed to be Greek, shouting rapid instructions to his boy and to the dock hands on the harbour side. There was no rolling of eyes or theatrical gestures, and Sarah was about to remark to Greig that he was a different person when he spoke his own language – but then she stopped herself, afraid that he might tell her it was all an act put on for the tourists. She would rather keep her illusions.

They were quickly under way, and Jorkos stepped up into the tiny wheelhouse which was rather like a sentry-box with a glass front and no sides, and from there he gave Sarah a running commentary on everything they saw. There were lots of birds, and at one point Jorkos

10

told her that there were seals alongside but she was not quick enough to see them. When they were outside the harbour, Jorkos gave the wheel to his boy and went round to collect the fares, and then came back to stand by the wheelhouse and smoke and continue his commentary. He told them some interesting things, and even Greig had now put away his book and was listening and looking about. On the horizon there were silver and green streaks which were islands of various sizes. Small fishing boats with red-brown sails sat still on the quiet blue water, their tarry hulls kissing their own images in the mirror of the sea.

The blue water slapped and chuckled under the *Ariadne*'s sides, and little waves turned over with a thin froth of white foam. They saw cormorants fishing, and further off a seal stuck his head up out of the water and looked like a human in a bathing cap. Above them the sun blazed in a sky even darker blue than the sea, paling to silver on the horizon, and the light danced on the blue water like diamonds.

"There, that is my island," Jorkos said suddenly. Sarah looked ahead and saw the mound on the horizon, and felt a surge of excitement.

"It's lovely," she said sympathetically, although they could not see it yet.

"Yes," said Jorkos simply, and then he looked at her and must have read the sympathy in her eyes, because he smiled in a quite different way, without any theatricals, and said, "You will haves a good time. If you want anything, you come to me. I am Jorkos Anastassiou – Jorkos is George in English. You can call me George if you like."

"I shall call you Jorkos," Sarah said. He nodded.

"I work for Mr. Geralds at the Villas, and I run the boats, and I am here and there. Anything you wants, you ask for me. Everyone knows me. I tell you the best places to go, where to see, where to eat, drink. You ask for Jorkos."

"I will," Sarah said. "Thanks." She smiled, and he smiled back in perfect understanding. She certainly had the best seat on the boat after all, and to make it perfect, she saw that the young man who had taken her place in the bow *had* got soaked after all, for no matter how still the sea was, the bows occasionally smacked into a rogue wave, and then the spray tipped over the bows and drenched the person sitting nearest. She gave him a grim little smile of triumph when he glanced back, and after that he kept his eyes to the front.

The island grew on the horizon to a tangle of green and white, and they caught a glimpse of golden and white beaches, and then the boat rounded a cliff topped with greenery, and ran into the little harbour. The stone slipway ran down from a neat grey harbour-front. Beyond, there were small whitewashed houses, dazzling in the sun, some with brightly-striped awnings, others festooned with purple jacmanna and vivid pink bougainvillea as if they had been decorated for a jubilee. The whole thing was enchanting beyond belief. Sarah turned to Greig with her eyes shining.

"Oh, it's *beautiful!*" she cried.

"You'd better tell your friend," Greig said, and there was the tiniest hint of coldness in his voice, but Sarah was too thrilled and excited to notice it. In a moment they had run up the side of the slipway, the boy had jumped lithely ashore and, catching the bow-rope, took a hitch round a bollard and took the way off her. *Ariadne* berthed sweetly with hardly a bump, and in a moment Jorkos had jumped ashore too to help his passengers out, while the boy and some other helpers attended to the luggage.

"Please wait just here, and I will takes you all up to the villas. Luggage will be brought up after you. Please be standing just over there," Jorkos bellowed his instructions, and the holiday makers formed an obedient crowd on the quayside.

"Is it far?" Greig asked as he climbed ashore, ignoring the hand Jorkos held out to help him.

"No, no, just a step – up there, on top of the cliff, no distance. Two minutes only walking."

Then there was only Sarah, and he reached down his brown and hairy arm and cradled her elbow and eased her up out of the boat as if she were something extremely precious and fragile.

"Don't forgets," he told her, approaching his mouth to her ear and speaking in a hoarse and extremely audible whisper, "you just asks for Jorkos."

In conjunction with the way he was holding on to her, it must have looked rather odd, for those nearest her gave a few muted laughs, but Sarah merely smiled and fell in beside Greig as Jorkos strode to the front of his group and waved his arm for them to follow. The boys were loading the luggage into a donkey-cart, and he bellowed a few commands at them, to which they responded with a wave and a grin. The holiday makers shuffled off in the big man's wake, with Greig and Sarah in the rear.

13

"Isn't it marvellous?" Sarah said, bursting with happiness. Greig only grunted, and she at last noticed that he was not as chirpy as he ought to be, even making allowances for his natural reserve.

"What's up?" she asked. "Seasick?"

"No – but I was nearly sick anyway, with your behaviour."

"What?" Sarah was too astonished to be angry or hurt. "What are you talking about?"

"Making up to that awful greasy man," Greig said in a low, angry voice. "Making a fool of yourself in front of all those people. Why did you have to play up to him? Don't you know his sort? There's always one, and they pick on the most gullible of the tourists and give them no peace. With you encouraging him like that we'll probably have him hanging round us all week."

"Greig, have you gone potty?" Sarah asked, perhaps not quite tactfully.

"No, but I think you have. Now for heaven's sake don't encourage him any more. The damage is done, but if you keep your eyes off him we may get away with it. You were behaving like an idiot."

"I was being friendly, which is what I usually am when someone is friendly to me," Sarah snapped.

"Friendly! Gazing into his eyes as if he were some film star asking you to marry him!"

"Oh don't be ridiculous!" Sarah shouted.

"And keep your voice down please – we don't want everyone listening to our private conversations – at least, not any more than they already have."

"You're being ridiculous," Sarah hissed, keeping her

14

voice low but injecting it with as much energy. "How can you possibly be jealous of a man like that? He's very nice, but – well really, he must weigh twenty stone! For heaven's sake be sensible."

"I am not jealous," Greig retorted, but some of the heat had gone out of his tone. "Don't be stupid. I simply deplored the way you let him smarm all over you and take you in. And I simply asked you to keep him at a distance in future."

Now that his voice had returned to normal, Sarah's anger dissolved, and she began to laugh again. She slipped an arm affectionately through Greig's.

"You were jealous, you nut. Like that time I went to the office party. I don't know whether to be flattered that you love me enough to be jealous, or offended because you're jealous of someone as impossible as that."

"I tell you I was not jealous," Greig said, but he kept hold of her arm.

"All right then, you weren't jealous." She smiled sideways at him, and fluttered her eyelashes coyly. "You dear old jealous nut."

And Greig grinned unwillingly, and squeezed her arm.

"I hope this hotel isn't far," he said. "I want a shower and a long, cold drink."

CHAPTER TWO

The villa lay at the end of a drive velvety with white dust, at the top of the hill and on the crest of the short brown cliff they had rounded in the boat not long before. It was a low building, two-storied in parts, in others simply a sprawl of one-storied annexes. The main frontage faced them as they arrived, and Sarah's first feeling on seeing it was that it had been worth the journey by 'plane and boat and foot. It was painted a curious shade of very pale pink that Sarah labelled to herself 'marshmallow', and the shutters, folded back like butterfly's wings, had faded in the sun from green to a silvery grey, rather like the colour of the olive-groves behind it. A verandah ran the length of the front, and it was weighed down with bougainvillea, heavy with its magenta trumpets.

A small, parched lawn fronted the building, and there were plots of flowers cut out of it, geraniums of more different colours than Sarah had known existed, and roses, crimson and white and scarlet and deep gold, their silky petals packed tight and their scent pervading the air with a maddening sweetness. All around, making it into a kind of clearing, were trees, tall dark cypresses and thorns on the seaward side, terraced olive groves behind, rustling

16

their tinfoil leaves, lemon and tangerine trees and bushes of prickly-pear. The branches were alive with birds like tiny moving jewels, but their song was drowned out by the insistent sweet-sweet of several million cicadas.

Sarah almost clasped her hands – it was that kind of moment.

"Isn't it beautiful!" she said, and felt the full inadequacy of that word.

"It is," Greig agreed without emphasis. He was not given to transports of joy, and Sarah knew that he was more concerned that their accommodation was going to be comfortable than that the first sight of the villa was like a step into a fairy story. Confirming her judgement, Greig went on, "It doesn't look very big, though. I hope the rooms will be all right."

"If it's small, it's more likely they'll take good care of each of us," Sarah said.

"That doesn't follow – " Greig began, but broke off as a man came out from the main door and crossed to the top step of the verandah. He was tall, distinguished, greying and immaculately suited in white – he could only be an Englishman.

"I won't keep you more than a minute, everybody," he called out, gathering the group's attention. "I just want to say welcome, and that I hope you have a very good stay here, and that if there's anything we can do to *make* it good, I'm the person to come to. I'm Gareth Hunter and I'm the owner and manager, and if you have any complaints – I should say, in the *unlikely* event that you have any complaints" – everyone laughed – "please come straight to me. At the reception

17

desk inside here you'll always find a member of my staff, and they'll be glad to give you any information you want, about places to visit and local transport and so on. And I would like also to draw your attention to the notice-board in the reception area, on which you will find various items of interest from day to day. We do hold one or two functions for the guests as a group, and while, of course, you're free to attend or not as the fancy takes you, I must say that you'd be fools to miss them." More laughter. "And now I'm sure you're all wanting to get to your rooms so I'll stop talking. Please come inside."

He turned and led the way into the cool darkness of the villa. Greig made a face at Sarah, nodding towards Gareth Hunter's back, meaning *are we going to be organised?* and Sarah made one back which meant *of course not, don't start.*

There was a pleasantly noisy confusion in the reception area until everyone had their keys and baggage and had been directed or led to their rooms. Greig followed his usual plan and waited with Sarah on the edge of the mill until nearly everyone else was dealt with, before drawing attention to himself.

"Ah yes, Miss Foster and Mr. Chapman," said a remarkably pretty girl whose white dress showed up the depth of her tan. "You're over in the cells – cells as in monastery, I hasten to add, not cells as in prison. Just in case you get the wrong idea." She grinned and showed her white teeth, and, taking a swift glance around, added, "Everyone else seems to be taken care of, so I'll take you there myself."

18

"Thank you," Greig said. "I think that's our luggage over there."

"It would have to be," Sarah muttered. "Everyone else has gone." Greig pretended not to hear. He took one case and the receptionist took the other, and led the way through a door on the other side of the hall. It led straight out of the back of the villa, and they found themselves facing a square lawn with a fountain in the middle of it, surrounded on all four sides with a covered walk like the cloisters of a cathedral. The main villa building formed two sides of the square, and the other two sides, obviously more recently built, had identical doors at regular intervals. The receptionist led the way to one of these doors, and threw it open.

"Here you are," she said to Sarah. "Cell number three. You're next door in number four, Mr. Chapman. You can see why we call them cells, can't you? Except that the view from the windows is lovely. All the windows are on the other side, so they're lovely and cool in the summer, as well as having the marvellous views."

"It looks lovely," Sarah said, stepping inside. It was quite plain, like a monk's cell in that the walls were painted plain white and were without decoration, and the floor was quarry-tiled, but there the resemblance ended. There were geranium red curtains at the window, and the bed was covered with a red and blue striped 'native' rug, which matched the rug on the floor. The furniture was plain pine – dresser, wardrobe and chair – and there was a small sink unobtrusively in the corner, and a mirror on the wall above it, and that was all. It was cool, and clean, and pleasant, and the air that flowed in through the open window was deliciously scented.

"It's absolutely – " she searched for the right word – "delightful. Thank you – I'm going to like it here."

"I certainly hope so. Well now, there's a bathroom at each end of the verandah, and the bar and dining room are just off the reception hall." The girl smiled at each of them in turn. "Is there anything else you want to know? Anything you need?"

"Nothing, thank you. Nothing for the moment," Greig said.

"Here are your keys, then. Bye for now!"

Sarah went across to the window of her room and called to Greig.

"Come and see! Just look here – you can see the sea!"

Greig joined her by the window and looked out. "You certainly can. And I can see the beach."

"Can you? You're taller than me. What does it look like?"

"White. White as a bone. I wonder if the villa has its own private beach."

"I'm dying for a swim, aren't you?"

"And some sunshine – I must say it looks tempting."

"Yes – sunshine. I'd like to get the sun on my hair – it's gone quite dark since last summer," Sarah said, catching up a long blonde hank to inspect it. She had naturally blonde hair, but the drawback to that was that only the sun could keep it bright, for she was too vain to dye or bleach it artificially. "It's almost toffee coloured," she went on, and stopped abruptly as Greig's hand closed over hers, drawing the shining strands through

20

his fingers. She raised her blue eyes to his grey ones, and smiled.

"You look very pretty standing there in the sunshine. I hope I'm not going to find you too distracting this holiday."

"I hope you do," Sarah retorted. "It is a holiday after all – you're supposed to be distracted."

Greig let her hair go and moved away, and Sarah was sorry she had spoken in that particular way, even while, at the same time, she was cross with him for being so mulish.

"We've had all that out," he said.

"Yes, we have," Sarah countered quickly, "so don't let's get into another argument. What about that swim?"

"Nothing doing," Greig shook his head, and for a moment she thought he was in a huff, until he looked back at her, smiling, from the doorway. "I'm going to dump my bag, and have a quick wash, and then – the longest, coolest drink this place can provide."

"What a good idea," Sarah laughed dustily. "And while we're about it, a bit to eat wouldn't come amiss."

"And *then* the beach."

"You're on! Meet me at the door washed and changed in ten minutes."

Sarah washed off the grime of the journey and slipped into a cream coloured linen dress, looking forward to the time when her tan would be as professional as the receptionist's and she would be able to wear dead white. She brushed out her long straight hair and pinned back the front two wings with hair slides, put on a pair of flat sandals, and went out to meet Greig. He had conceded just so much to the occasion and no more – he was jacketless and tieless, but otherwise was dressed much as he would have been on a warm day in England.

"Going native?" she teased him, but he didn't catch the joke. They found the bar easily enough, and discovered that most of the guests had had the same idea, and were sitting or standing around in groups talking amicably. Their host, Gareth Hunter was there, on a high stool at the bar, and the pretty receptionist who had shown them their rooms, and Sarah guessed that it was owing to them that the group was so much at ease.

"What would you like?" Greig asked her as she took in the scene with half a smile on her face.

"I don't know, really. Everyone seems to be drinking Pimms, so I might as well go along with the crowd. It looks about right for the occasion – cool and festive at the same time."

"Just as you like," Greig said, "though as far as I can see there's not much drink there. They might as well serve it on a plate with a knife and fork."

"Don't you believe it," Sarah laughed. "Many's a nice young girl has been sneaked up on from behind by a Pimms too many. It packs quite a punch of its own when you're not looking."

Greig wasn't to be tempted by her recommendation, however, and came back with cold lager for himself and "one wet salad, as ordered."

"Thank you darling. How romantic." She glanced round. "Let's go and join Mr. Hunter and see what he's got to tell us about the island," she said, and moved off towards that end of the bar before Greig could protest.

22

He did not like meeting strangers himself and would have stayed diffidently in a corner all his life if it weren't for Sarah's occasional rebellions.

"Hullo! Come and join us," Gareth Hunter said as she caught his eye. "Rooms okay?"

"Yes, lovely, thanks. I like the way you've built round the square like that – only it's rather a shame to have that lawn and fountain shut away where no-one can see it."

"Ah, there's a reason for that," Gareth said. "Is this your first time in Greece?"

"Yes."

"Then you wouldn't know. But it's the only way we can keep a decent bit of grass about the place. Nice for lying out on when it's too hot to go down on the beach. You'll find as you go round the island that most of the grass is beginning to turn, and by midsummer our little bit by the fountain's the only green grass left."

"We were wondering about beaches," Sarah said, catching up the cue neatly.

"You couldn't have come to a better place," Gareth said seriously. "There are lovely beaches all round the island, and all safe for swimming. We have our own private beach, of course – if you go out of the front door, and follow the path round to the right, you'll come to some steps cut into the cliff, and they lead down to our beach. Oh, while we're on the subject – " he looked round to gather the rest of the group into the next sentence, "wander round here as nearly nude as you like, but please don't go down to the village in swimsuits. The villagers are rather strict about that."

"What's the village like?" someone asked, and another voice put in,

"What's the night-life like?"

"Well there's nothing very much in the village, of course, except a few cafes and two tavernas, and the mobile cinema on Thursdays. We make our own entertainment pretty much up here – music and dancing and anything else that happens to happen."

"Do things 'happen' very much?" Sarah asked with a smile.

"Wait and see," he twinkled at her. "Dinner tends to turn into a party once we get to know each other and the ice is broken. There've been times when none of us have even got around to moving from the dining room to the bar."

"It sounds fun," Sarah said.

"It is," he confirmed. "That's the nice thing about the villa, the way it brings people together." As he spoke his eye rested on Greig, who had said nothing at all and was standing almost behind Sarah as if to distance himself from the conversation. Gareth smiled and tried to bring him into the group. "Is this your first holiday in Greece too?" he asked.

"My first time in Greece, yes. But it's a working holiday for me. I have to do a lot of work in the next two weeks. Exams coming up," he added to Gareth's politely raised eyebrow.

"I shouldn't bank on that," Gareth said with a laugh, but Greig didn't join in.

"I *have* to bank on it," he said. "And my room seems nice and quiet."

There was nothing more to say about that, and as Sarah felt the leaden words hit the floor at her feet a wave of exasperation swept over her. Wouldn't he even *try*? It was necessary to remove them from the group before everyone's face froze over.

"How about sampling the beach now, Greig? Will you excuse us, everyone? Let's go and have a swim."

She turned quickly to move away and almost ran into the insolent young man, who was standing practically on her heels and probably, she thought, listening to her conversation. He smiled knowingly at her, as if, she thought, he pitied her for being trapped with Greig. But no – he couldn't be thinking that. Wasn't it her own thought that she was passing off as his? It made her feel vaguely guilty, and she dismissed it hurriedly.

Her feelings of anger and guilt died away very quickly when faced with the glorious prospect of the white beach and the blue, blue sea, and left her feeling only happy and relaxed. They had a brief swim in the milk-warm water – neither of them felt very energetic after the long journey – and then slipped shirts over their shoulders and went for a walk along the beach. Sarah had a new swimsuit with her, but she didn't put it on for this occasion, feeling that it was so gorgeous and outrageous it needed an occasion all to itself for its first outing.

The sun was going down and it was beginning to grow cool, though it was still as hot as a good summer day in England. The angle of the sun gave a new significance to things, throwing them into sharp relief and giving the eye restful shades on which to linger after the flat brightness of the day. Greig was an ideal companion on a quiet walk, for he didn't talk much, but listened equably when you wanted to say anything. They walked to the end of the white beach and climbed up the low cliff at the other end, and found themselves on a narrow white path which wound its way through a scattering of stunted trees over the cliff top and eventually down into the next bay.

On their left was the sea, its colour darkening to blue-green as the sun lowered. Now that some of the brightness was gone from the air, it was possible to see other islands on the horizon, some of them looking near enough to swim to.

"I'd like to go out to some of them," Sarah said. "I wonder if Jorkos does boat trips?"

"You've only just got to this one," Greig said, "and now you're wanting other islands."

"Well," she smiled, "you've heard about cows and the grass on the other side of the fence."

"I don't know about greener, but nothing could be bluer than the sky we've got here," Greig said, looking up at it. "I wonder why blue is such an attractive colour to the human eye? Or perhaps we think it's an attractive colour because we associate it with fine weather and therefore with feeling good. Which means that if red skies were the norm, we'd feel the same way about red."

Sarah's attention dropped off during this and they walked in silence until the path began to drop towards the next bay.

"Perhaps we'd better not go too far," she said. "It seems to be getting dark – well, getting dusk, anyway. And I'm hungry."

"Yes, I am too. We didn't have anything to eat before we came out as I suggested."

"Perhaps we should start back. It might be dinner time, with any luck."

They turned and retraced their steps, pausing only to look from time to time at the brilliant, blazing sunset that was going on like a full-scale technicolour spectacular over the sea, now on their right.

"If everything's going to be like this," Sarah said, "I shall be emotionally exhausted all the time. I'll need a holiday to get over it."

"You'll get used to it," Greig said. "In a week's time you won't even notice the sunset."

"Heaven forbid!" Sarah said, and then, happily, "Isn't it marvellous to think we've got two whole weeks more!"

"Yes," Greig said, and she realised he was thinking about his damned exams again. He dropped her hand which he had been holding, and she was upset, not because he had dropped it, but because she had not been aware that he was holding it in the first place.

CHAPTER THREE

Sarah woke the first time, very early, to the realisation of
bright young sunshine and birdsong, and with an inward
smile dropped off again. Her neat little bed in the neat
little 'cell' was divinely comfortable, and she slept for
another couple of hours to wake to stronger sunshine and
the first impression of heat.

At once she sat up, stretched, and climbed out of bed
to look out of the window. The sky was a lighter shade
of the same Aegean blue as yesterday, and there was
a sense everywhere of freshness and anticipation that
made her catch her breath and want to hurry outside
to see what was going to happen to the day. Besides,
she was not quite able to shake off the inbred English
sensation that the sunshine would not last, and that she
should therefore waste no second of it. A quick swim
before breakfast perhaps? A glance at her watch told her
it was only just after seven, and breakfast was not served
until eight – plenty of time.

She grabbed her towel, hesitated, and then picked out
her new swimming costume. She had intended to save it
for a ceremonial first wearing when she went to the beach
with Greig, but on second thoughts she decided that it

might be as well to baptise it first, so as to make sure it fitted properly and didn't fall off when she swam. She was rather doubtful, in any case, as to whether Greig would receive it as it ought to be received, for it was very bold and very revealing. It was red with white spots, a nominal one-piece since the top was connected to the bottom with a narrow strip of material. There was virtually no back to it at all, and precious little front, while the design made it look from the side as if she was wearing nothing at all.

One of Sarah's – in her own opinion – few good points was that she had a good figure and really nice legs, and she had fallen in love with the ridiculous, lovely costume on first sight and thought she looked rather noticeable in it. Greig, however, with his peculiar, unreasonable jealousy, might well think she looked too noticeable.

"Well," she said to herelf, "he's jealous when there's absolutely no cause whatsoever, so it really can't make things any worse." And so she had bought it, and brought it with her to Greece concealed under her old, more modest, blue one.

She put it on now, easing the scraps of material into the right positions on her body, and wishing that she was tanned so as to set it off properly. She dragged her long fair hair carelessly back and tied it with a scrap of chiffon at the back of her head. Then she slipped on the towelling bath robe she had brought with her to serve the dual purpose of dressing-gown and beach-robe, shoved her feet into a pair of flat sandals, grabbed her towel and went out.

It was quiet as she went through the main building, but she could hear in the distance the murmur of voices and the soft chink of china and cutlery which told her that the staff were up and probably preparing breakfast. As she stepped outside the sun fell on her for the first time, and she felt its pleasant warmth through the coolness of the morning air, a feeling that she was to associate ever afterwards with Greece. She left the marshmallow-pink villa with its carnival decorations of bougainvillea, and trotted along beside the wild fuchsia hedges to the steps in the cliff that led down to the bone-white beach. There is something particularly pleasant about a beach early in the morning. The angle of the sun throws the sand into relief and picks out cool shadows where later in the day there will be only dazzle. Where the sea had been there was a strip of shining clean sand with no footmarks. Sarah kicked off her sandals and felt the sand burning and then cool as she sank through the fine top layer, threw off her robe and felt the air cool then warm as the sun touched her. Her costume quite forgotten, she ran down to the water's edge in rapture, broke through the first incoming waves and then threw herself down into the water's warm embrace.

At home the water would have struck icy at the first plunge, but here it felt only pleasantly cool – even at this time of day it was tepid. The waves were small and brisk, rolling past her with no flurry of foam, but an air of going somewhere and having no time to waste. Sarah swam slowly out from the shore with a strong breast-stroke that gave her the chance to keep her head up and look around her. Something black in the water made her pause, and she stopped and trod water to watch what turned out to be a pair of cormorants fishing. They regarded her cautiously each time before diving, but evidently had little to fear from humans.

The knowledge that it was nearly breakfast time made her cut short her swim, or she might have gone on for ever, and she turned and swam quickly in, ran up the beach to where her belongings were left in a neat pile, and started to dry herself briskly. It was when her head was buried in the towel as she dried off the ends of her hair that she first realised that she was not alone on the beach.

"That's a lovely costume you're nearly wearing," said a voice that sounded vaguely familiar. Sarah jerked her head up in surprise and saw the young man sitting a little way from her, idly pouring sand from one hand to the other and looking at her with the same expression of half-mocking admiration that had annoyed her the day before.

"You might knock before you speak," she said with an effort to sound cool. "You startled me."

"It was mutual, I assure you," he said, showing his nice teeth as he smiled. "That bikini is one that, in the common parlance, would knock your eye out."

"It isn't a bikini," she said, annoyed, and turned her body slightly so that he could see the joining strip. His smile broadened slightly. "And I don't particularly relish personal remarks on my appearance, thank you," she added sharply.

"If you wear things like that in public, you're bound to get remarks," he said, still tipping the white sand from one palm to the other. She noticed, despite herself, that he had quite a respectable tan already, and wondered what he did to achieve it. Perhaps he worked outdoors? But no, she told herself with a sneer, he probably used a sun-ray lamp at home.

"Why don't you mind your own business? What right

31

have you to be rude to me? This beach was empty when I came down – I hardly call that 'public'."

"My dear Miss Foster," said the young man, standing up and straightening his face to a formal solemnity, "I do assure you that I didn't mean to be rude. That was the *last* thing on my mind."

"How do you know my name?" she asked, sidetracked by curiosity. He smiled again – he seemed to smile very easily: in fact one got the impression he found any other expression difficult to maintain.

"It was very easy. I watched to see what room you went to, and then I looked it up on the register. Miss S. Foster. I was very glad to see it was 'Miss', despite the presence of Mr. G. Chapman."

"My fiancé," she said loftily, and then, "We're engaged."

"That usually follows," he agreed solemnly, and she blushed for her own stupidity.

"So you know all about me? Well, as I can't change that, I suppose all I can do is to try to even up the score," she said.

"I won't put you to that trouble," he said quickly. "My name's Alec Russell. How do you do." He held out his hand and Sarah took it automatically, even while she was thinking it was an odd, formal thing to do when you were standing on a beach engaged in verbal wrestling, and one of you was nearly naked.

"That puts you at an advantage now, you see," Alec Russell went on. "Because you know my first name and I only know yours begins with an S. And as for knowing all about you – I haven't even begun yet."

His words, and the way he looked at her, made a strange

shiver run down her spine, and she used it as an excuse to get away.

"I must get back – it must be breakfast time," she said, pulling her robe round her quickly.

"I expect it is," he said pleasantly. He hesitated as if he wasn't sure whether to walk with her or not, and then he stopped and let her go on without him. He called after her, however, when she had gone a few paces, "If I might presume to give you some advice – "

Sarah stopped and turned unwillingly. When people *presumed* to give you advice it was usually their way of disguising an unpleasant opinion they wanted to impart.

"I don't know if I'm teaching you to suck eggs, but even if it makes you late for breakfast you should have a quick shower before you dress. The salt on your skin attracts the insects, you see, and you'll be bitten all day if you don't."

She relaxed, glad that it had been no worse than that. "I would have any way," she said, "but thanks for the tip all the same. 'Bye."

"Goodbye. See you at breakfast," he called after her as she ran up the steps.

The shower after the swim was delightful, and Sarah didn't want to hurry out of it, so she was late for breakfast, and found Greig already seated, an empty place beside him for her, and a meticulously-folded newspaper beside his plate.

"Hullo," she greeted him, and got in first with, "I see you managed to get hold of a newspaper. Is it an English one?"

"Yes – only the Telegraph, I'm afraid, but it's better

than nothing. Apparently that Hunter chap has them brought in by boat from a shop on the mainland that has them flown over from London every day."

"It must cost the earth," Sarah wondered. "It seems like an awful lot of trouble for something very unimportant."

"It is of the greatest importance," Greig assured her sternly. "Just because you are the most appalling igno-ramus and never read any kind of newspaper it doesn't meant to say that no-one finds them of any value."

"Well, I know how much you rely on your paper at home," Sarah said with lazy good humour. "It's like a drug to you – you can't get through the day without it. But I would have thought since you were on holiday – "

"Being on holiday makes no difference – " Greig was beginning when suddenly Sarah leaned forward with an exclamation of surprise and snatched the paper from his hand.

"But it's yesterday's!" she cried. She looked up at Greig with dawning delight in the absurdity. "This is yesterday's newspaper!" and she began to laugh while Greig struggled to maintain his dignity. "I would have thought you'd have something better to do with your holiday than spend it reading old newspapers." She shook her head. "You really are absurd."

"As I said before, it's better than nothing. I suppose it must be the only time in one's life when one will settle for an old paper – when one's abroad," Greig said, but he stopped trying to read it anyway, and when she gave it back to him he folded it still smaller and stowed it under his seat to be read later when he wouldn't be mocked for it. He decided to open a counter-offensive.

"You were out early this morning," he said. A waitress came over to give them the breakfast menus, and reading them gave them an excuse for not looking at each other.

"How do you know?" Sarah asked.

"I knocked on your door to see if you were awake, and you'd gone."

"Actually I woke up very early, and it looked so delicious outside I decided to go down to the beach for a swim before breakfast." The menu for breakfast was simple and delicious. She decided at once to avoid the usual run of cereals that were only too familiar, and try some of the local delicacies.

"Alone?" Greig shot the single word at her while apparently as completely occupied in his own choice.

"Of course alone," said Sarah, trying not to sound irritable at the inevitable question. "What did you think – I had an assignation at seven in the morning?"

"You don't need to snap – I only asked a simple question."

"It isn't the simple question I mind, it's the way you ask it."

"Sorry I spoke."

A plateful of bread was brought, white bread with a crisp golden crust, and they both were glad to help themselves and break it and spread it with butter. It gave them something to do. Their first course was brought very quickly – cornflakes for Greig, and goat yoghourt for Sarah, and a pot of coffee. There was a little stone jar of local honey on the table, and Sarah mixed a spoonful of that into the yoghourt and found it delicious. Her spirits rose. The coffee was powerful and aromatic and delicious, and she drank it black. Her spirits rose still further.

Greig meanwhile crunched his way without interest through his cornflakes. Sarah had for a long time suspected that he had no real interest in food, and would have been happy enough if the science-fiction world of eating only pills really existed. It was another small chasm between them, for she loved food, loved cooking it almost as much as eating it, and was looking foward to extending her experience while she was there.

"You didn't think to call for me, then," Greig said suddenly, and Sarah was forced to bring her mind back from the realms of Greek breakfasts to early morning swims.

"No, I didn't," she said, and since he seemed to be expecting more she went on, "I thought you'd still be asleep. I know how you like to sleep in in the mornings. Anyway, I was quite happy to go for a swim alone. I don't mind being alone."

"I see," he said. They ate in silence. Their second course was brought – eggs and bacon, toast and marmalade for Greig; a plate of buttery scrambled eggs and fresh fruit for Sarah. She tried eating peaches and grapes with the eggs and wondered why she had never thought of it before. And she would finish off she thought, with another chunk of that delicious bread, spread with honey. She was just manoeuvering a piece of peach onto her fork when Alec Russell came into the dining room, looking freshly bathed in white shorts and a blue short-sleeved shirt, his hair damp from a swim or the shower or both. As he passed their table he smiled at Sarah and said good morning, and she turned her head after him, thinking how smart

36

he looked and wishing Greig could bring himself to dress like that.

"I didn't know you knew him," Greig said and she turned back to look at him resignedly. She knew what was coming.

"I met him on the beach this morning."

"I thought you said you were alone."

"I said I *went* alone."

"To meet him?"

"I went for a swim, and he came down to the beach just as I was coming back up. We exchanged a few words, that's all."

"Why?"

"What do you mean, why?" she said, her temper rising. "He's a guest at the same hotel, for heaven's sake. I'm not an arab woman, to go round in a mask and never speak except to my lord and master."

"Of course not," Greig said, trying to sound reasonable. "It just puzzles me that the only people you ever seem to talk to are good-looking young men."

"Oh do stop it, Greig," Sarah said wearily, and then tried to lighten the tone, for she was no longer enjoying her delightful breakfast. "I'm sure he'd be flattered to hear you calling him good-looking."

"Don't you think he is?"

"It never occurred to me one way or the other."

"You turned round to have a second look at him just now," Greig said, slightly mollified.

"I was looking at his clothes, actually," Sarah said truthfully, "and wished you'd take to dressing more casually. In your off-duty time, I mean," she added, seeing a homily about suits and accountancy hovering on Greig's lips.

"I don't see myself running round Wimbledon in shorts," he said, smiling. The mental picture his words called up brought a grin to Sarah's face.

"I'd give a lot to see that," she said. "Pass the honey, will you – all this fresh air's giving me an enormous appetite."

After a leisurely breakfast they wandered out onto the verandah where a number of the guests were loitering and smoking or chatting to each other. There was a sensation of peace and ease that was almost tangible in the crystal clear air, and the voices discussing what they would do today sounded as if it didn't much matter what they did, or if, indeed, they did anything at all.

"I was thinking" Greig said, leaning his weight on the verandah rail and admiring Sarah, who was facing him and basking in the sun, "that it would be a good idea if I did my work in the afternoons. I imagine that it gets pretty hot after mid-day around here, too hot to do anything much. I expect they all have siesta time here, as they do in Spain and Italy – the locals I mean. I could retire to my room then and work until the evening meal, and then relax during the evening."

"If it's too hot to do anything, how will you manage to work?" Sarah asked.

"Oh it will always be cool enough in those rooms. They keep the shutters closed while the sun's round that side. Didn't you notice yesterday how cool it was in there?"

"Hm," Sarah said non-committally. If he got up late, as he liked to, and started work at mid-day, it didn't leave him much of the day with her. Still, looking at him now and seeing how much more relaxed he was already, she hoped that the air and atmosphere would work its magic on him in time. Not that she wanted him to fail his exams through lack of study, but she was sure that he would get through them anyway, for he was the most conscientious of students at other times, and she felt that his desire to study during the holidays was just his pernickety nature going to extremes.

"Well," she said at last, "I'm glad you'll take the evenings off, anyway. But I want to get about and see the island, and some of the other islands too, if I can. We won't be able to do that if you're studying from noon onwards."

"I'm sorry," he said firmly, "but I must stick to a timetable. Why don't you go on your own? You said you didn't mind being alone, and there'll probably be other people from the villa going on trips that you could join up with."

"But – " Sarah began in surprise, and then stopped herself, realising what he was about. He wanted to make up to her for the scene at breakfast, by pointedly encouraging her to go off alone, proving that he trusted her and admitting that he had been silly. He was smiling at her warmly now, and she responded by crossing to him and tucking her arm through his. "What a good idea," she said easily. "And maybe if you get plenty done you might feel like joining me later in the week." Which was her way of saying, I'd sooner have you along, but I understand your point of view.

The crowd on the terrace was dispersing gradually,

some heading off towards the beach and others towards the shady path down to the village.

"Since you've already been to the beach once today," Greig said, "how about a stroll down to the harbour? We could have a look around, a bit of exploration, and maybe find out about boat-trips for you at the same time."

"An excellent idea," Sarah smiled. "And perhaps also we could have lunch at one of those little cafes where you sit outside in the sun at wooden tables, before you come back to work?"

"Sounds just right. Shall we go?"

CHAPTER FOUR

Their walk round the village only scratched the surface of what Sarah felt sure there was to see, for by the time they had got ready to go and walked down the hill it was mid-morning, and Greig's noon deadline was drawing near. Under the striped awnings facing the harbour were one or two obvious tourist shops – 'bazaars' they called themselves – selling postcards and souvenirs. Sarah could guess that these were the usual cheap tawdry things that most tourists get trapped into buying, but they were still far nicer than their equivalent in other countries she had been to.

Greig would scarcely let her even look at them, so scared was he that she would waste her money on something not worth while, and he was continually tugging at her sleeve, both actually and metaphorically, to get her away from the alluring displays. Had he been able to realise it, she was not in any danger of being hooked here, for she was certain that there were shops packed with goods twice as delightful in more hidden places behind that bright harbour front and she was saving her money until she could squander it elsewhere. It would

41

have done no good to tell Greig that, though – it would only have worried him more.

"All those handbags," she sighed as Greig led her away towards a cafe. "And the rings! They're very much cheaper than they are at home, you know. It would be well worth buying some things here to take back."

"It's only your first day," he said coaxingly. "If you spend all your money now, you'll be sorry later when you've nothing left."

"I'll always be sorry when I've nothing left," Sarah said solemnly, "but as for not spending now – haven't you ever just wanted to buy things? And buy them *now*? Later just isn't the same." She glanced up at him and smiled. "No, I can see you haven't. You always plan ahead, don't you. Even for little things like buying souvenirs."

"Yes, I do – even for that," Greig said, and he looked down at her with a suddenly troubled look, as if he'd just thought of something. He stared at her long and earnestly, but her attention was elsewhere at that moment and she didn't notice it. By the time she looked at him again, he was his usual self, apparently having settled his thoughts back into their usual groove.

They took their seats under a red-and-white-striped umbrella at a table outside a cafe, and Sarah laughed at Greig pretending not to notice various other people from the villa seated at neighbouring tables.

"It's no good, you know – you're going to have to make friends with some of them by the time the holiday's over," she whispered to him.

"Don't bet on it," he whispered back. "What do you want to eat?"

42

"Oh, nothing much, in this heat. I'm sure they don't eat big meals in the middle of the day out here."

"The only place in the world where they eat a big meal in the middle of the day now is Lancashire," Greig said.

"Why Lancashire?" Sarah asked, and they wrangled about it peacefully until their order arrived. They ate bread and cheese and olives, and drank wine watered to a delicate pale pink. A bowl of fruit was set on the table too, and Sarah looked at it with melting eyes.

"Oh look at that fruit!" she exclaimed. "Did you ever see anything like it?"

"No," Greig said. "The bowl is beautiful, too, isn't it? I think it's olive wood. I'd like some wooden bowls and things like that in my house when I finally get one."

"Well I should think that this is the place to buy them," Sarah said, and she stopped short as she realised that Greig had said 'my house' and not 'our house'. It was nothing of course – just a manner of speech, and yet it sounded so odd, as if she were a stranger to his private life, not as if she would be sharing it with him. She reached out absently for a nectarine.

"You'd better wipe it first," Greig said warningly, "or better still peel it and throw away the skin. You don't want to spend the rest of the holiday in the bathroom, do you?"

Sarah sighed. "You could take the romance out of anything, do you know that? If you'd been Romeo you'd have been calling out to Juliet that the balcony rail wasn't safe to lean on." And Greig laughed and patted her hand.

'Unusually well said for you."

"Cheek."

When they had idled through their meal, Greig said that it was time for him to go up and start work. Sarah groaned at this.

"I don't know how you can even think of it," she said. "That wine – even well-watered – and all the sunshine and fresh air have made me deliciously sleepy. The very thought of work makes me want to put my head down."

"You always did have a weak head," he said affectionately, ruffling it with one hand. "But there's no reason why you shouldn't put it down for a little while. It would probably do you good, actually, to have a short rest now."

"What, and waste all this sunshine? I can't quite shake off the thought that it will disappear at any moment. But you're right, of course. I'll have a short zizz on my lovely comfortable bed, and then pop down to the beach later."

"When it's cooler – not until two thirty at least," Greig said sternly.

"Yes Daddy," she said meekly, and he gave her an affectionate shove. They walked up to the villa together, and parted on friendly terms at the doors of their respective rooms, after Sarah had extracted a promise from Greig that he would join her on the beach if he finished his afternoon's work early.

"But don't bank on it," were his parting words to her. I don't, she thought to herself as she flopped gracelessly onto her bed. How lovely, she added, to be able to sleep in the middle of the day if you want to. Poor people back home, at work in nasty stuffy offices! If I were at home, what would I be doing now? I'd just be walking down the street to the sandwich bar to buy one of their horrible plastic sandwiches, done up in cling-film, and a polystyrene cup of instant coffee, and the woman behind the counter would be whining 'Eat here or take away?' . . . And thinking of the lovely contrast with what might have been, she fell asleep.

Although Sarah was not a methodical person, one of her abilities was to wake when she wanted to, and having decided to sleep until two-thirty, she was not at all surprised to wake exactly at that time. For a moment she could not think where she was, since she had never slept in the middle of the day since the time she was in hospital to have her appendix out. The room was still cool, but her eyes felt gummy, and she was glad to go across to her little wash-basin and sluice her face with cold water. Her next thought was a longing one for the sea, and in a matter of seconds she had donned her costume and grabbed her bits and pieces and was heading for the path to the beach.

Although there were quite a few people on the beach, it was not at all crowded. She smiled hello at those she passed, and noticed, not without smugness, that one or two had made the mistake of sitting out through the hottest part of the day and were already an ominous pink across the shoulders. She made her way further along the beach to where a spit of broken rocks edged out to the sea and there she dropped her belongings and sat down on the hot white sand to admire the view while she attended to her hair.

She had not put it up before she came out, and she

preferred not to leave it loose while she swam as it was terrible if it got soaked in brine – there was so much of it. She was still a little sleepy from her snooze, and had twice gathered up the long heavy mass and twice dropped it to be scattered by the little breeze when a voice she now recognised spoke up from behind her:

"It reminds me of the story of the goose-girl. Did you ever read it?"

Sarah turned her head sharply and opened her mouth to reply but Alec Russell held up his hand urgently for silence, and said with a comical expression of alarm,

"No no, don't speak! Wait, wait a minute!" and he began hunting around in the sand at his feet with exaggerated gestures.

"What on earth – ?" Sarah began, but he stopped her again.

"No, don't speak. Just a minute – ah, here we are!" He straightened up with a stone in his hand, with which he tapped sharply on the rock against which she was leaning. "There," he said, and regarded her with an expression of expectation.

"What are you doing, you idiot?" Sarah asked, trying not to laugh at his expressive face.

"The last time we met – on this very beach, I might add, you told me to knock before I spoke. So, I knocked."

"Did I?" Sarah said, laughing.

"You did. But it seems the occasion is not remembered by you as clearly as it is, alas by me." He passed a hand across his brow. "Spurned, spurned," he muttered, and struck his breast with a tragic fist.

"Oh do stop it, everyone's staring," Sarah told him.

46

"It's you they're staring at, your hair. I told you it's like the story of the goose girl."

"I don't know that one."

"Ignorant," he said pleasantly. He sat down facing her, cross-legged on the sand, with an easy grace that Sarah admired. "She was really a princess, you see, and she had beautiful long golden hair which she used to comb out every day while she watched the geese. And the peasant boy who had been set to help her was fascinated by it, and every time she let her hair loose he would come and stare and try to touch it. The goose girl didn't like that, so every time she would summon up the wind to snatch away the peasant boy's hat, and while he was chasing it she would get her hair combed out and done up again."

Sarah considered this. "Every day?"

"Every day," he confirmed.

"Then he was nuts," she said firmly. "Why on earth didn't he just put his hat in his pocket, or keep hold of it when the moment came?"

"Do you know, I've always wondered that too. Out of charity to the poor peasant boy, let us suppose she always took him unawares. Or that he didn't connect her hair with the sudden gusts up to force five. After all, who would?"

"Well, I still don't feel sorry for him. If he cared all that much he would have let his hat go instead of chasing it."

"Perhaps it was his only hat. He was very poor, you know." Sarah looked sceptical. "But the point of the story is not the lack of intelligence on the part of the boy, but that the goose-girl's hair was so beautiful that he couldn't help staring at it. And wanting to touch it."

47

And as he spoke he slowly stretched out his hand towards Sarah's loosened hair, and she suddenly recollected herself and drew back slightly, upon which the young man let his hand drop. She had thought of Greig, wondering what he would have thought if he had walked in on such a crazy conversation, and thinking of him made her self-conscious and she blushed.

"I really must have a swim," she said quickly, standing up. The young man stood up with her and smiled, but without intimacy this time, simply a friendly smile.

"Good. I was just going in myself. Looks good, doesn't it?"

Sarah coped with her hair in one or two practised movements, and set off down the beach with Alec Russell beside her, but with just enough distance between them for it not to look particular. The sea was just brushing the shore, lapping over and barely withdrawing: the little breeze that was playing on her shoulders seemed to have no effect on it. They stopped at the water's edge and looked out.

"You should see it at night," he said. "The phosphorescence is amazing, like green fire."

"Really? I should like to see that," Sarah said, unable to imagine it. "How do you know about it? Have you been here before?"

"Once, last year in fact. I don't often go to a place twice – not as close together as that, anyway – but it was so lovely here – " he broke off, thinking of its beauties. Sarah was about to remark that Greig, by contrast, liked only to go to places he'd been to before, but she stopped herself in time, aware that it would be as impolitic to mention Greig to Alec Russell as vice versa.

"Did you come alone last time as well?" she asked instead. He gave her a sidelong glance.

"What a prim question for a young lady. No, I am not married, which is what you really wanted to know."

"I didn't think you were," Sarah said, blushing.

"Nor even engaged to a fiancée, Miss Foster, so now you know."

"I have no interest in your private life," Sarah said loftily. "I merely asked because – " she couldn't think of a creditable reason and so finished honestly, "well, it was for something to say."

"That's honest at least," he said, and turned to face her. Sarah found herself noticing what a nice mouth he had, narrow but curly, and really lovely teeth. She was particular about teeth . . . "But I hope we never have to talk just for the sake of talking. Or that we'll ever find it hard to find something to say to each other."

Sarah's eyes were held, but her mind was a confusion. This must stop, she was telling herself. It was all wrong for him to be saying things like that to her in a voice like that, and for her to be, even momentarily, believing them. She remembered Greig's strange slip of the tongue that morning in talking of 'his' house as if she would not be in his future; and now here was this complete stranger (not a stranger at all, an inner voice said) talking as if their futures lay together. She dragged her eyes from his face, turned away and began to walk, as if casually, out to sea, while casting around in her confused thoughts for something to say that would restore normality.

"I pity all the people at work today," she said, almost at random. "Think of typewriters and telephones on a day like this."

"I can't think of anything I'd rather not think of," he said easily, keeping pace with her. "You should fix your mind on beautiful thoughts, Miss Foster."

"Greig's working this afternoon," she blundered on, forgetting her earlier resolve.

"Greig?"

"My fiancé."

"Ah!" He paused. "Very worthy of him." In a moment of insight, Sarah realised he had been picking his words with care, and it amused her. She chuckled.

"He's a very worthy person, in every respect," she said.

"What a lovely sound that was," Alec interrupted her.

"What?"

"That sound you made. A low laugh, I think they call it in books. Half way between a pigeon and a siamese cat."

Sarah was a little more braced against his language by now. "We were talking about Greig," she said sternly.

"We were? I thought it was only you."

You could read that two ways, she thought. Why am I still here listening to this sort of thing? she wondered at herself. It's all wrong. I should have given him a cold answer and walked off up the beach long ago. What would Greig think if he saw us together like this?

But despite her thoughts, she continued to walk slowly

through the milky-warm water. When they reach thigh-deep water they turned parallel with the shore and walked towards the outcrop of rocks.

"Greig has to study each day because his exams fall almost immediately when we get back from holiday," she went on. "They're very important to him."

"More important than you?" he asked.

"It isn't a question of that," Sarah said, and was about to explain more, when she caught herself up. "Anyway, he's working every afternoon while we're here."

"Leaving you alone to explore the island?"

"I suppose so."

"Playing right into my hands," he said. "This is where I give an evil chuckle and an aside to the audience. I must say I think it's jolly good of him to leave you unsupervised."

Sarah turned abruptly to face him. "Look," she said, "you really mustn't talk to me like that. It isn't fair."

"Fair to whom? No, don't answer. I'm sorry. I won't do it any more. Though why didn't you send me packing with a flea in my ear if you thought I was some beach Romeo making a nuisance of himself?"

"I didn't think you were like that."

A pause in which Alec Russell regarded her more seriously than she liked. "You're very right," he said quietly. "I'm not like that." Another pause, this time slightly awkward, and then he said in a cheerful voice, "Have you noticed how clear the water is? You can see right to the bottom, look!"

Sarah did, seeing her own legs strangely distorted and whitened by the refraction of the sunlight, and her feet, now partly covered by the sand, for they had been standing still for a while.

"Oh, look at the fish!" she cried, for there were three small silver ones bumping their flat faces at her legs – touching and then backing off just enough to bump again. "What are they doing?" she asked. "They're just like cats 'weaving'. Aren't they sweet?"

"They're feeding," Alec said. "Oh, don't look so nervous – they aren't after your flesh! It's just the salt on your skin."

"I would have thought salt was the one thing they had enough of," she said, whispering as though the fish might hear and be scared off.

"Different sort, I expect."

"Well I prefer to think they're just being friendly," Sarah said firmly. "It's more romantic."

"Perhaps they are," he said. "Many of the things we do have more than one motive. Who can say what goes on in a fish's mind when it nibbles a lady's leg?"

Sarah snorted with laughter at his phraseology, rippling the water enough to scare the fish off. "Oh," she said, disappointed.

"Plenty more where those come from," he said. "Let's go over to that rock, and I'll show you some of the pretty things that grow under the water. What we really need is a couple of snorkels, then we could just drift along with our faces under. I wonder if we could buy them or hire them in the village?"

His words made Sarah realise that they were getting too intimate again, and in a kind of panic she backed away from him, and began to stammer.

"I have to be getting back now, I'm afraid. It was very nice of you – "

"What's wrong?" he asked, seeming genuinely puzzled.

"Oh, nothing's wrong," she said reassuringly, but casting a glance over her shoulder as if Greig might have crept up behind them. "It's only that – well, I must go."

He looked as if he might ask more, but then seemed to change his mind. He nodded to her, said, "See you at dinner," and dropped suddenly into the water, swimming away from her with a powerful crawl out to sea.

Sarah watched him go, and realised that he had done it so that she could, if she wished, stay here enjoying the sun without compromising herself. It was nice of him, she allowed, because the last thing she actually wanted to do was to leave the beach and the water and go back to the villa just then.

Greig called for her before dinner time and asked her to come and have a drink in the bar before the meal. He looked fresh and smart and not at all as if he had been working all day.

"I'll just get changed, and meet you in there," Sarah said. "Five minutes, okay?" She had already showered and had been lounging on her bed reading while she waited for the dinner bell, so she only had to slip on a dress and do her hair. Greig had obviously made an effort with his appearance and dressed for the evening, and she felt she could hardly do less, so she picked out a backless frock of a deep turquoise material which looked and felt so much like silk that she didn't mind at all that it was only a polyester. She drew her hair to the top of her head and tied it with a ribbon of almost the same colour, and let it cascade down to her shoulders. A plain gold choker finished the effect.

Greig stood up for her in his meticulous way when she came into the bar, and his eyes were not the only ones that looked at her.

"You look lovely, darling," he said, and she knew at once from his voice that he was feeling pleased with himself.

"Thank you. Did your work go well?"

"Yes. I'm very happy with this afternoon's progress," he said. "If I get as much done every day I shall be in a very sound position for the exams." He ordered her drink from the barman and then turned to her again. "I hope you weren't too bored on your own?"

"Oh no," she said happily. "I don't think I could ever be bored here."

"What did you do?"

"Just swam and sunbathed on our own beach. And then I came back to my room and showered and lay on the bed reading while I cooled off."

Greig wrinkled his nose. "Sounds pretty dull to me," he said. "Is that all you're going to do while you're here?"

"I wouldn't mind if it was," Sarah admitted, "but I was looking at a notice in the vestibule as I came back from the beach. It seems there's a half-day trip to a bay round the other side of the island tomorrow in the afternoon. I was thinking of going on that." She looked at him doubtfully. "I s'pose there's no chance of you coming too?"

He shook his head firmly. "Sorry. I must stick to my timetable. But you go. Maybe make friends with some of the other villa people, as I know you're dying to."

Sarah ignored the gentle gibe. "The only thing that bothers me is that there are bound to be places to visit that will take a whole day, and what will we do then? If you stick to this studying in the afternoons – "

"Well I daresay I could make an exception once or twice, but I'd like to see first how I get on for the first few days. If everything goes as well as it did today – "

At this point Alec Russell came into the bar, and his eyes went as directly to Sarah as a pair of homing pigeons. Greig didn't miss the look, and he stopped talking and his smile tightened on his mouth. Alec's eyes went on past Sarah and he nodded to someone beyond her, in the corner, towards whom he began to walk. But as he passed Sarah and Greig he gave the latter a friendly nod, and to Sarah a smile, saying,

"Good evening, Miss Foster. Had a good day?"

Sarah, embarrassed, only nodded, and he passed on. Greig waited until he had gone and then said in a low voice.

"He knows your name." Sarah nodded, a little wearily, fearing a scene.

"He looked it up in the register. He knows yours too."

"He didn't use mine," Greig said.

"Well he told me he knows it. Now Greig – don't start."

"I wasn't going to."

"Let's at least have a happy evening, together."

"Yes, let's," Greig said, and he looked at her in a strange way, perhaps speculative, perhaps sad, but if Sarah noticed it, she put it down to his inward battle with his jealousy. "Another drink?"

"I don't think so. I'd like to have some wine with dinner, and I don't want to end up pie-eyed." She smiled as she spoke, and Greig squeezed her hand to show her that it was all right again.

CHAPTER FIVE

The boat trip was advertised as starting at twelve the next day, and when she put her name down for it Sarah was asked if she wanted a packed lunch to eat on the boat.

"It's quite a long sail," the girl said, "and it's pleasant to eat on the boat under the awnings. Otherwise you might not get anything until you get back to dinner in the evening."

"Oh yes, I'd like that," Sarah said. "I've no qualms – I'm a good sailor."

"No need to worry about that," the girl laughed. "It'll be as calm as a mill-pond – as usual."

She and Greig spent the morning on the beach, and walking along the top of the cliff on which they had walked on the first day, and at half past eleven they parted at the villa.

"Don't bother to come down the hill and see me off," she said, going on tiptoe to kiss him goodbye. "I'll see you at dinner – or in the bar beforehand if we're back early enough."

"All right. Have a good time. Have you got everything? What about this packed lunch?"

"They give it to you on the boat. I've got my camera

57

and my swim-suit and a book in my bag here, so that's all I need."

"Well, enjoy yourself," he said again, and he looked rather wistful. Sarah wondered if he might want to come with her after all, but she didn't feel she ought to tempt him by asking, if he had made up his mind to work instead. "You look very nice," he said finally.

"Thanks," she said. "Well, see you later, then."

As she walked down the hill she mused that he had been complimenting her quite a lot recently, which was very nice for the ego, but fairly unusual for Greig. Perhaps the Greek sunshine was beginning to work on him. She was very casually dressed for this trip, in ordinary jeans, and a short-sleeved cheesecloth shirt that ended just below her bust, leaving her midriff bare. She had flat sandals on; as usual, her hair was held back from her face by her sunglasses pushed on top of her head, and over her shoulder she carried her faded old denim shoulder-bag, and her camera. "Every inch a tourist," she thought to herself, but she was comfortable.

Down at the harbour it was not difficult to pick out the boat as it was already half full, but she was surprised for she had half expected it to be the old *Ariadne*. This boat was larger and newer, in shape pretty much like the Thames pleasure barges, with all the passenger space forward. It was freshly painted white, and the passenger deck was shaded by a scalloped blue awning. The name painted on the bow was *Penelope*, and putting two and two together over this, she was not surprised to find that it was Jorkos holding the clip-board and marking off the passengers at the foot of the gangplank.

"Ah, you have comes," he greeted her with dignity. "Good, good, we will have a good trip, and you shall see my beautiful island. What you thinks of my boat? Isn't she beautiful, my little *Penelope*?"

"Very pretty," Sarah said truthfully. Jorkos looked over her shoulder with a puzzled frown.

"He isn't with you, your brothers? He isn't coming?"

"Who?" Sarah looked round too, as if she might see who he was referring to. "Oh, you mean Greig? The man I came over with?"

"Sure, him. He isn't your brothers?" Jorkos' eyes were innocent of guile.

"No, he's my fiancé."

"No – honest to God, I thought he was your brothers."

"You're kidding me."

"Honest – I see he's too young to be your fathers." Still Jorkos didn't smile, and Sarah was forced to leave it at that, still not knowing if he was teasing, or if she and Greig really presented such a picture to the public.

The boat left the slipway promptly, with a good crowd on board. Jorkos had more helpers with him on this larger boat, and they scurried about in response to his shouts. As soon as they were under way, two of them began to dispense the lunch-packs, each one in a neat brown bag, drawn from a large hamper. Those who had been taking photographs of the harbour quickly found themselves seats to be able to eat in comfort, and Sarah, feeling hungry, took hers and made her way forward to satisfy her previously thwarted urge to sit in the bow. The crowds cleared as people sorted themselves out, and at once she caught sight of Alec Russell standing with his own lunch pack in his hand, looking about him as if lost. She resisted the urge to call to him. He looked nice – not in the same way as Greig, but cool and casual in blue denim cut-offs and a blue and white striped tee-shirt. She had not noticed before the reddish tone in his dark-brown hair. It must be the shade that brings it out, she thought. Then he turned his head and saw her.

He smiled and came straight over, as if it had been she he was looking for all the time.

"Hello. You've got the best place there – glad to know you can take care of yourself when you're alone. You are alone, I take it?"

"I was," she said. "But I'm not now, am I?"

"Not if you'll allow me to join you, Miss Foster?"

"It's a free boat – I can't stop you."

"You could if you wanted to – do you?"

"No. Please join me. Why do you keep calling me Miss Foster?"

"It's all the name I know. Better than calling you Miss Jones, isn't it?"

She laughed. "I should have picked up the hint before. I thought you were just being funny."

"I like the way you say 'just' being funny," he complained, "as if it were so easy. It takes a lot of skill to be funny all the time, without being vulgar."

"I didn't mean it that way. Anyway, what would you like to call me?"

"Is there a choice? What about telling me what S. stand for?"

"Sarah."

"May I call you Sarah?"

"Yes. May I call you Alec?"

"Yes. I prefer it to Sarah." He sat down beside her.

"Idiot."

"Ah, I like that – that means we're friends," he said, looking at her with a satisfied air. He sighed with comfort and stretched his legs out, and rested one brown forearm along the gunwale of the boat. Sarah noticed that the hairs on it were golden, bleached almost white by the sun.

"Where did you get that lovely suntan?" she asked. He glanced down at himself modestly.

"Oh this? In a bazaar in Calcutta, actually. It's second-hand – got it dirt cheap. You'd never guess it, would you?"

"You are funny. When did you decide to come on this trip? I didn't see your name on the list when I booked."

He looked alarmed. "I hope you didn't sign up for that reason alone. Imagine if you'd booked up solely to get away from me, and I pursue you like an avenging fury!"

"But you still haven't answered me," Sarah interrupted his flight of fancy.

"Oh I signed up as soon as I saw your name on this list. With no Mr. Chapman. Where is he, anyway? Studying again?" She nodded. "Poor soul," he said, and he sounded genuinely sympathetic.

"Jorkos thought he was my brother," Sarah said.

"Who's Jorkos?"

"Oh, the man who owns the boats. You know – over there, with the cap on. I couldn't make up my mind if he was joking or not."

"Probably."

"Probably which?"

"Probably both. Shall we have some lunch?"

"I'm starving. I hope this packed thing is all right," Sarah said, dubiously. "I remember when I was in the Isle of Wight on School Journey the packed lunches were always spam sandwiches, as dry as sand."

"I suppose you ate them with *desert* spoons," Alec quipped, and they both sniggered. "Anyway, this is a far cry from a school trip to the Isle of Wight. And I can predict almost exactly what you'll have in that lunch pack."

"Try, then," Sarah encouraged him, pulling open the mouth of the brown bag.

"Bread, cheese, and olives," he said promptly. "It's all anyone ever has for lunch here. Well, am I right?"

"I'm not sure," Sarah said, "I haven't got it open yet."

"Are you absolutely certain you're not sure?" he asked her.

"Positive," she said, straight-faced. She dipped into the bag and brought out bread, two sorts of cheese, and olives, and their eyes met, and they laughed.

"Now then, Miss Smith," Alec began, sounding like a detective inspector on an old-fashioned radio play, "you may or may not have noticed that I am carrying a large plastic carrier bag."

"I'm afraid it slipped my notice, inspector," she said meekly.

"That's all right, Madam," he said generously, "the general public aren't trained to be observant of small detail the way we are in the Force."

"Get on with it," she prompted him. "The commercials are coming up."

"Wrong station," he said in his ordinary voice. "Well anyway, in this carrier bag are some things I brought with me to make up the deficiencies of a packet lunch. I plunge the hand into the bag and bring out – hey presto! – a white rabbit!"

What he actually brought out was some of the delicious thin ham that was a speciality of the region. "Try it *with* the cheese, on the bread," he suggested. It was excellent.

He had also brought some cold lamb kebabs, and a plastic bag full of salad, and more bread, and they ate it together, dipping into the same bag, feasting on the simple, delicious food while the *Penelope* skimmed across the gentian-blue sea beside the fairy-tale coast of the island, and the sun edged round and caught in the fringes of their hair and made them squint their eyes not only with laughter.

And to end the feast he had brought fruit, including brown figs, split with ripeness and showing their pink tender bellies.

"I've never tried them before," she said, eyeing them cautiously.

"You'll love them," he promised. She did.

"I don't think I ever want to eat anything else but the kind of things we've been eating," Sarah said, sighing with happiness. "Or do anything else but sit here looking at the blue sea and the sunshine."

"Not even swim in the blue sea? Or walk in the sunshine?" he asked her cannily.

"Oh well, of course . . ." she said. There were other small islands on the horizon, coming and going mysteriously as the curves of the shore led their boat towards or away from them. "They look like little caskets full of treasures," Sarah said. "What do you suppose is packed in them?"

"Apes and ivory and peacocks," Alec said promptly. "And silk and spices, and white ponies with blue eyes, and parrots, and acrobats wearing gold bracelets."

"More likely to be Russian gymnasts wearing track-suits, nowadays," Sarah said straight-faced. Alec looked wounded.

"That's the trouble with you young girls nowadays – you've no poetry in you. No romance at all. I should have brought my paper with me."

Until that moment Sarah had quite forgotten Greig, and in enjoying this strange young man's company she had felt no twinge of guilt – nothing but a complete ease in her pleasure. But now she thought of her fiancé working away back at the villa, and of how upset he would be if he could witness the instant intimacy that had seemed to arise between her and Alec. He would be terribly hurt and jealous. He was never very expressive of his feelings to others – why, even Jorkos had thought he was her brother – but his feelings were no less strong for that.

Jealousy had always been one of his faults, if you saw it as a fault, and he had suffered on many unnecessary counts before now. If he were to see her and Alec behaving towards each other like this he would be terribly wounded, for he would never be able to accept that a friendship like that could exist innocently between a man and a woman. She felt no guilt in the friendship, yet knowing that Greig would think it guilty made her feel suddenly constrained. And she could not even tell Alec what was wrong, for she felt that it would expose Greig where he was weakest. He had never done anything to forfeit her loyalty. She could not do otherwise than defend him, with or without his knowledge.

A silence fell between them which, though not unfriendly or awkward, was a little restrained, and Sarah resolved to part company with him when they put in at the next harbour. Being together on the boat, where they could scarcely avoid each other, was one thing – but sight-seeing in his company all afternoon, when there was a whole island to explore, she somehow felt would be a kind of unfaithfulness to Greig. Not that there was anything other than sheer friendship between her and Alec Russell – of course not! – but it didn't matter so much what was the case but what Greig would think was the case.

As soon as she decided that, the uneasy feeling left her, so she knew that she was right. Another person's jealousy could make you feel curiously guilty, and your feeling of guilt made them all the more jealous. Far better to avoid anything of that kind, and behave as if they were present all the time.

After a slow boat-journey of about an hour and a half they reached their destination, and the *Penelope* put in at a small harbour very much like the one they had just left – so much like, that Alec and Sarah exchanged an amused look, both thinking the same thing, that perhaps the whole trip had been a hoax. It was obviously a larger village, however, for there were many more shops along the harbour front, and more people, and more dogs. The water-front was quite busy, in fact, and Jorkos was hailing people in his fog-horn voice, exchanging what sounded like friendly insults with the fishermen and other workers as they passed.

Some of the people were obviously waiting for the boat, two of them to help her dock, and others to pounce on the trade in the form of passengers disembarking. One man had a barrow of fruit which he was wheeling into position where they would have to pass it; another had set up a camera on a tripod at the bottom of the gangplank, and was preparing to snap people as they came off the boat.

Everyone began to push forward towards the gangplank, and Sarah joined the gentle press, with Alec just behind her.

"Not waiting till the crowd eases then?" he murmured to her as they inched forward, and she blushed at the reference and wondered if she ought to say anything to him – but she didn't want to make an issue of it. He didn't mean to offend, only to amuse. However the words stuck in her mind, and she began to debate with herself how she should part with Alec Russell on the dock-side, firmly enough to make him understand she meant it, but without being rude. What reason could she give which would convince without offending?

Their turn came, and as the gangway was two people wide, Alec walked down beside her. Her eye caught the photographer at the foot, and as her attention was taken from what she was doing, her mind already being elsewhere, she stubbed her foot against one of the treads and stumbled.

She gave a little cry of alarm as she pitched forward, and she might have had a bad fall had not Alec moved like lightning and caught her in both arms. He swayed with the impact but regained his balance, and for a moment she was held close against him, their faces only inches apart. Her heart was beating fast with the sudden scare, and if she had paled a little, she now regained her colour. His arms were very strong, and held her firmly, surely more firmly than was any longer necessary? She found herself thinking how beautiful his features were, where before she had only thought him funny and pleasant – but his straight nose, finely-etched nostrils, his long mobile mouth were beautiful, and his dark eyes, so full of feeling, as if he were looking right into her mind, reading it – reading her heart –

And then the long eyelashes – surprisingly long for a man – lowered a little over the dark, feeling eyes, and his lips parted slightly as if he were catching his breath, and Sarah held hers too, trembling, as the moment seemed to extend itself into a timeless silence – where everything moved in slow-motion –

And then time resumed its course, and she was set back, unharmed, only a little shaken on her own feet. The incident had only taken a second or two – the rest was imagination. Alec was himself again, back from her a respectful pace, his face that familiar mixture of kindness and amusement that seemed to be its permanent expression, and he pretended to dust her off and joked cheerfully,

"Now who's talking about Russian acrobats?"

"I tripped," she said unnecessarily, walking on down to the bottom ahead of him. "Thanks for catching me."

"Every tumbler has to have a catcher. I am looking for a job, as it happens."

"Well I'll certainly give you a good reference," she said lightly, stopping once they were clear of the harbour-side and turning to him, "but I'm tumbling alone at the moment. Thank you for sharing your lunch with me."

He put his head a little on one side, a gesture that would have been whimsical from anyone with a less funny face than his. "That sounds a bit like goodbye."

"A lot like it," she said, trying to sound firm but managing only to sound wistful. "I have to explore on my own." Please don't ask me to explain her, eyes begged him. Please understand. This is embarrassing.

"Okay," he said with a small shrug. "I'll see you later, then, on the boat back. Don't get lost, will you? And don't forget the time."

A ragged smile touched her lips. "You sound like my father."

"All right. Have a nice time. That do instead? Good. Cheerio, then." And he turned and walked away, managing to make it look quite natural. You'd have made a good actor, she silently informed his back. And then she turned in the opposite direction and headed for the shops.

CHAPTER SIX

Almost as soon as she had parted from Alec, Sarah thought it was silly, and regretted it. It would have been so much more fun to wander round the village with him. She was sure that they would like more or less the same things, such as poking around the little shops, and with his rampant sense of humour, everything would have been amusing. She had never enjoyed anyone's company so much.

It was silly to feel guilty just because if Greig were here he would be suspicious. After all, if Greig were here she wouldn't, in all probability, even talk to Alec: she'd merely have said hello as they passed each other, and she and Greig would have gone off one way and Alec the other. But thinking of this made her realise that there surely ought to be something wrong in talking to a person she wouldn't talk to in Greig's presence. Wasn't that dishonest, underhand?

No, something inside her answered – it was because of Greig's strange temperament that she couldn't speak to Alec in his presence. She thought back over their conversation on the boat – there was absolutely nothing in it which she could not have said equally well in front of Greig, there was nothing she would not want him to hear. It was not she who was wrong, but Greig's jealousy. And Alec seemed to have somehow fathomed Greig, for he had never yet stopped to talk to Sarah when she was with Greig, even though he, too, never said anything that Greig might not hear.

But then, what about that moment when she stumbled on the gangplank? Yes, what about that? Sarah considered, and in thinking back felt her cheeks redden a little at the memory. Yes, had he seen that, he might well have thought something was up between her and Alec. That strange moment when they seemed motionless in each other's arms, their eyes meeting with that odd intensity: Greig might make quite a lot of that. But it *was* nothing, she reassured herself, just the momentary shock of nearly falling making her dizzy, that was all. It really was all.

Puzzling over these thoughts took her to the top of the harbour, and here she paused and looked about her, wondering where to go next. She hadn't really any heart for rummaging through the shops – that was a thing that had to be done in company to be much fun – and so instead she struck off up a path which led over the headland. The path wound amongst small clumps of trees, and between them was a lawn of short, springy turf, scattered with flowers. On her right hand was the sea, blue curling to white at the foot of a cliff of varying height, on her left the rolling greensward. It was an idyllic scene.

When she came to the top of the hill, the scene changed, for this part was bare of trees and was bearded instead with patches of dark green myrtle and purple-bloomed heather, and as she topped the rise saw, a little way off, a boy accompanying a flock of goats from one grazing place to another. They trotted along in their apparently haphazard way, leaping nimbly over hidden stones and ditches, and their little bells tinkled, the sound coming to Sarah clearly on the still air. She suddenly realised that she had not heard the sound of a motor car or an aeroplane since she arrived on the island. Enchanted place indeed! It was worth coming here, if only to get away from those two all-present noises.

The boy saw her, and raised a hand in greeting, and called "*Chairete!*" to her, and she waved back, smiling. The goats milled past her, staring up at her with their mad golden eyes, and as they disappeared over the rise and the quietness settled down again, she stood quite still and simply looked and listened. She heard chaffinches chipping away in the nearest clump of olives, and heard the silvery leaves rustling in the small breeze that came and went. There was a wood-pigeon, too, repeating his throaty, bubbling cry again and again, and the small lapping of the sea below.

This is the place to be, she thought suddenly – and this is a real holiday, the quietness, the absolute ease. No rushing, no hustling, no noise, no pushing and queueing and paying for this and that – just a hillside under a blue sky, and a little breeze. She understood why the ancient Greeks thought their Gods lived in places such as this. She decided suddenly on a swim, and on picking her way down the nearest low rock-tumble – it was hardly a cliff – she found a tiny beach of corn-gold sand all to herself, and the warm blue sea murmuring to her invitingly. And this was how she spent her afternoon – bathing in the

71

friendly sea, and basking on the golden beach, with no other companion than her book. Sometimes it's good to be alone.

At the end of a peaceful afternoon she made her way almost reluctantly back to the harbour for the return boat. She had so far sorted out her thoughts, albeit subconsciously, that she had almost forgotten the trip over with Alec, and had resolved to avoid his company on the way back, to ignore him hereafter as far as she could with politeness. She was in good time, for though the boat was there and ready, they had not yet put the gangplank down, and the rest of the party was waiting in groups or wandering around the harbour-front and making last minute purchases. There seemed to be some interest in a large board, set up like a notice-board near the embarkation point, and Sarah, not being without her fair ration of curiosity, naturally wandered over to it.

The board was covered with a sheet of polythene, and underneath it she saw there were pinned photographs, held at the corners with thumb-tacks, each with a number, bold in black on white underneath it. A further glance told her that these were the photographs the man was taking as the party came down the gangplank, together with some taken afterwards in the harbour. The idea was now obvious – he took the photographs when the party arrived, went back to his studio and developed and printed them, and then displayed them on the board in time for the returning party to examine them and give an order for prints. Yes, there was a price list, pinned fluttering at the bottom of the board; the numbers were simply to identify the pictures by.

As the crowd moved and she found herself nearer the front, Sarah was able to have a look at some of the prints. She could quite see why they would be popular – quite apart from the fact that one is always attracted to a photo of oneself. They did make good snaps, with the background of the blue and white boat, and the blue sea, and the green and white cliff that guarded the harbour; and in the foreground the smiling holidaymakers in their bright clothes coming in pairs and groups down the gangplank. It was a nice reminder of a lovely day – and then a horrible thought struck Sarah, and her mouth went dry as she searched the board.

With a lurch of her heart she saw it – number ten. The photographer knew his business, had pressed the shutter at the very instant that would make the best, the most damaging picture. Not that he could know that, of course – he was not to know that they were not holidaying together. There it was, a charming, not to say romantic picture. Alec's arms were round Sarah, her hands were on his shoulders, gripping them tightly. Her face was tilted up to his, with an eager, perhaps slightly startled look on her face; he was gazing down at her, and the lips of both were slightly parted as if they had been snapped in the split-second before a kiss. It was a lovely picture of young lovers: they were almost dressed alike too, in blue and white, blending in nicely with the background. The sun had caught the red tinge in Alec's hair, and Sarah's straight, long hair hung in a dazzle down her back, hiding Alec's hands.

Except that they weren't young lovers; except that it wasn't what it seemed – but who would believe that?

Sarah stared and stared at number ten, and a middle-aged lady standing beside her saw the direction of her eyes and looked too, and murmured "Lovely!", giving Sarah an indulgent smile. Sarah was not thinking lovely thoughts just then – she was thinking of Greig and what he would say – with justification this time – if he saw it. Horrors! He mustn't see it, of course. She must buy this print, and destroy it, tear it into tiny pieces and drop it over the side of the boat on the way back. It must not be seen.

Determined, Sarah wriggled her way backwards out of the group around the photographs and looked around for the photographer. Her wandering eye could not at first locate him, and then she saw him at a little distance, taking a picture of two giggling girls and a donkey, which was held by a patient small boy with bare feet. She could imagine, as she hurried over to him, the caption that would be inscribed under that particular photograph in the album – "Which one's the donkey?"

Quite naturally, the photographer was occupied with his job at that moment, and despite the anxiety which was making Sarah hop up and down on the spot, his attention could not be weaned from it. Out of the corner of her eye she saw that the gangplank of the *Penelope* was down, and that people were beginning to embark, and her agitation increased a point. However the giggling girls also noticed this, and at last kept still enough for the photographer to perform his task. The little boy with the donkey was paid and led the beast away, the photographer picked up his tripod and camera and turned towards the boat, and at last Sarah was able to engage his attention.

He was without doubt the oldest man she had ever seen.

His face was so dark brown with sun- and weather-tan that it was almost black, and his dark eyes, bright and small like a monkey's, were sunk into a network of wrinkles below two bushy white eyebrows that birds could have nested in. Sarah, trotting along beside him as he strode with surprising vigour towards the harbour front, gabbled out her request, and the old man turned on her an engaging smile that showed ancient gums innocent of teeth, save for one yellow ivory stump at each corner, like goal-posts. His attention was certainly hers, but his look and the smile he bestowed on her were of perfect and sublime incomprehension. Sarah drew her breath and tried again, more slowly.

"The photographs – on the board – " she said, pointing. His eyes followed her finger and he nodded, still smiling. "I want to buy one," she went on with more confidence. "Number ten – photograph number ten on the board. I want to buy it, and if possible the negative, although that doesn't matter so much as long as you don't make any more prints of it. You see – " She was just about to embark on an explanation of why she wanted the photograph, but she decided that it wasn't anyone's business, that it was better kept to herself, and that it didn't make any difference anyway. The old man was still looking at her, patiently if not expectantly, and she said instead, "How much is it, please?"

His expression did not change. Sarah pointed again at the board, and said "The photographs? How much?"

"Only five drachma," the old man told her in a piping voice. "Nice pictures. Five drachma only. Five drachma." And he displayed the fingers of one hand, in case she

75

should still be in any doubt. There were only one or two people left on the harbour, and it was necessary to conclude her bargain and get on board pretty quickly. She had no idea whether five drachma was a fair price or not, but she didn't much care – she only wanted to get hold of that picture and tear it up.

"I'll have it," she said at once. "Number ten, please. That one – " She pointed at it, since they were now standing beside the board. The old man smiled and nodded, but made no move to unpin it. "I want that one please," she said with increased agitation.

"Fine photo," he agreed, smiling monumentally at her. "Only five drachma." He seemed to sense there was some breach in communication between them, and furrowing his brow in thought he spoke a sentence in rapid Greek at her, and pointed at the boat, repeating it. Then, with an obvious effort, he said.

"At hotel. Photo at hotel. Five drachma."

Sarah's expression rivalled his. Suddenly remembering Jorkos, she said, "Wait – I'll be back!" And ran towards the boat. Jorkos would come and translate for her, perhaps even conclude the bargain, for she had an idea that the Greeks liked to argue over the price, and it might be that in repeating 'five drachma' the old man was trying to induce her to make an offer. She ran nimbly up the gangplank, almost the last person aboard, and pushed through the crowd on deck looking for Jorkos. She wouldn't have thought a man of his size and volume would be hard to find, but he must have been below with the engines or in the crew's cabin, out of sight, for she couldn't see him. A lot of thudding an rattling drew her attention back to the entry port, where she saw, to her horror, two young boys pulling up the gangplank in preparation for sailing.

"No, no, you mustn't!" she cried out. "I have to get back on shore. I want to buy a picture from that man." The two boys smiled at her and continued their task. They too, spoke no English. Desperately she cast her eyes around, and with great relief saw Jorkos, like a massive, hairy, guardian angel, picking his way nimbly along the catwalk outside the taffrail towards them.

"Oh, Jorkos," she called to him in anguished tones. "Tell them to put it down again! I have to go back on shore."

"What's the matter, Miss?" he asked her with fatherly concern. "You left somethings behind? Don't worrys, I come here all the time – I get it back for you. What you lost?"

"No, no, it's not that. It's just that I have to buy one of the old man's pictures, but he doesn't seem to understand, so I wanted you to explain to him that I want to buy it."

Jorkos laughed hugely. "He understands all right, don't you worrys. But you don't buys it here – no time. He brings the pictures round to the villa, puts them on the notice board, then you gets all the time you wants to look, and buy any you want. The pictures will be there tomorrow mornings, first thing."

Sarah's mind boggled at the thought of that picture being pinned up on the notice board for all to see. "But you don't understand," she gabbled. "I want that particular one. I have to have it. I don't want to buy it at the villa – I want it now."

Jorkos shrugged sympathetically, although he evidently had no idea what was wrong with his passenger. "No time now, Missy," he said. "We gots to gets back for dinner. Don't you worry, the photos will be there tomorrow. No-one going to buy it till then. Anyway, Costos make as many pictures as you want – you only gots to pay for them."

And with that he turned his attention from her fascinating problem to the more urgent business of skippering his boat. Sarah turned away with despair, wondering if there was any way in which she could avert the disaster. She could hardly hang around in the villa's lobby, waiting for the photographs to arrive. Greig would be bound to want to know what she was doing. If they arrived early enough, before breakfast, say, she might be able to intercept them, but if it was any later than that, Greig would be with her anyway. Perhaps she could have a word with whoever was behind the desk. It would mean explaining the matter, but most of those young girls looked pretty understanding and though it would be embarrassing, she had nothing to be ashamed of. Yes, that seemed to be her best hope. Otherwise she'd just have to brazen it out – but Greig would never believe her.

Sunk in these gloomy thoughts, she did not notice the ship making her way out of the harbour, nor did she noticed the approach of her former companion until his voice broke in on her brown study.

"Hello – you don't look too happy. Something up?"

She looked up, and his pleasant smile did nothing to abate the sparkle of anger in her blue eyes.

"You know perfectly well there is. You can go away

78

and stop bothering me – you've done enough damage already!"

He lifted his hands and his eyes in surprised innocence. "What have I done?"

"Don't give me that! You must have seen the photograph."

"Oh, that," he said, enlightened.

"Yes, that," she spat. "So don't try to look innocent."

"But how is it my fault?" he asked reasonably. "I didn't ask the man to take the blessed thing."

"No, but you must have known he was there, taking pictures."

"Of course I did. So did you."

"Well – "

"Well what? What should I have done? Let you fall? You could have broken your leg. In any case, one doesn't debate whether or not to let someone fall down – there isn't time. One just grabs them. It's instinctive."

"Yes, I know, I know you saved me from a nasty fall, and I'm grateful for that," Sarah said in a more reasonable voice, "but you didn't have to – well," she paused, wondering how to put it.

"Yes?" Alec encouraged her.

"You didn't have to look so – you shouldn't have made me – " She was getting more and more confused, and as her cheeks grew redder, the concealed smile on his long curly mouth grew more and more obvious.

"Yes? What was my mysterious crime? What did I do?"

"Oh, blast you, you know perfectly well what you did!" she shouted at him. One or two people turned to stare, and

79

she lowered her voice and tried to look calm. "Can't you imagine what would happen if Greig saw that photograph. He'd never believe that you'd only just caught me from falling down."

"That, my dear girl," he said with a grin, "is entirely your problem. You'll just have to make sure he never sees it, won't you."

"Yes, but how, is the problem. Jorkos says the man brings the prints up to the villa and displays them there so you can order what you want. They'll be put up on the notice board tomorrow."

"I can foresee a sleepless night for you tonight," Alec said with a charming lack of sympathy. She could see he didn't take her problem at all seriously. "Never mind," he said, "at least let it be said that the condemned woman ate a hearty supper. Eat, drink and be merry, for tomorow – " and he finished off with a hideous throat-cutting gesture.

"Oh shut up!" Sarah said irritably.

"No, no, I'm serious," he said. "You might as well make the most of your last day. I've got a bottle of wine here in my plastic carrier bag – " he lifted and shook it. "Have a drink with me, and tell me how you spent your day, and I'll tell you how I spent mine."

"I want nothing more to do with you," Sarah told him loftily. "You've got me into trouble enough. I don't even want to speak to you."

Far from upsetting him, this only seemed to amuse Alec. So much for her worrying about offending him! She moved away from him, as quickly as the people on deck would allow her, and took her place up in the bow. She leaned over to watch the water creaming along under her, and to

80

get the cooling spray on her hot cheeks, and while she was still in this position, Jorkos came across to her and asked her with tender concern.

"You not sick, Missy?"

"Oh, no of course not," she said hastily, straightening up. "Who could be sick on a boat as smooth as this?"

"My brothers, he gets sick just looking at the sea," Jorkos told her gloomily. "He only has to walk down the jetty, and he gets sick right away."

"I suppose he makes sure he never goes near the water, then," Sarah said, thinking that it was most unfortunate to be a poor sailor when you lived on a small island.

"He's a fisherman," Jorkos told her with sad relish. "My brothers Christos has ten children and a wife and a mother-in-law to keep, so he has to go out every day. And every day he's as sick as a dog, soon as he sets foot on his boat." He made a vivid pantomime of his unfortunate brother's daily trouble. "I tells him Christos, you are a saint, to do this for your family, sick every day and never a day missed. You know what he says?"

"No," Sarah said, beginning to sound amused.

"He says, Jorkos, I gots ten children. A man has to pay for his pleasures." And he laughed heartily, licensing Sarah to join in. Out of the corner of her eye she saw Alec hovering just behind the big man, waiting his opportunity to get into the conversation. She searched around for something to say, and remembered something she had seen while hanging over the side.

"Jorkos," she said, "What's that eye painted on the

81

prow for?" Just under the name an open eye was beautifully, delicately painted in blue and black and gold on
the white prow of the boat.

"That's the eye of the god," Jorkos told her. "It looks
out for us, keeps us safe and brings us home. Without that
we would have no protection. All the boats have the Eye
painted on. You look when you see another boat."

"Yes, I've noticed that before," Alec said, having
wormed his way in on Jorkos' other side. "All the fishing
boats in our harbour have them. And all the boats are
painted black, except for yours. Why is that?"

"I paints mine whites for the tourists – looks prettier,"
Jorkos said, including him with Sarah in his conversation.
"The other boats are all painted black because it don't
show the dirt so much. You don't haves to paint them so
often."

He remained with them for the rest of the return trip,
telling them little anecdotes about the islanders and the
visitors he had escorted and legends and traditions, some
of which Sarah was sure he had made up. But he was
good company, and she was so fascinated that she quite
forgot her resolution not to speak to Alec, and they had
a very pleasant three-way conversation. It was only when
the boat reached their harbour and Jorkos was called
away from them in his official capacity as skipper that
she remembered the trouble she was in and became silent,
and Alec fell silent in sympathy.

"I'll see you tonight," he said to her cheerfully as they
prepared to disembark.

"I doubt it," said Sarah. "I shall be spending the evening
with Greig."

"Ah, yes, but didn't you look at the notice-board this morning? Dinner tonight is to be a barbecue party, and there'll be dancing and drinking until all hours. So we'll be all mucking in together, and we're bound to see each other."

"'See' in the literal sense, perhaps," Sarah said, and she felt a twinge of unease as she thought she detected a gleam of wicked amusement in his eyes. He was planning something, she was sure, and much as she would rather not know what it was, she had the feeling that she would be finding out all too soon, and to her discomfort.

CHAPTER SEVEN

To Sarah's surprise, Greig was on the slipway to meet the boat as she pulled in. There was no-one else there, apart from the usual dockside loungers whose whole existence seemed to be helping boats in and out, and Greig looked so obviously foreign, so single and out-of-place, that he struck her suddenly as a lonely figure. He had spent his afternoon alone in his room working, she thought, while she was enjoying herself. She had been alone too, but she was not pitiable in that. She wondered suddenly what it was like to be Greig, to be so reserved and to find it so hard to enjoy oneself, and for a moment she overran with sympathy for him. Then she shook herself and thought how dedicated he was to his work, and told herself that he enjoyed it, that that *was* his way of enjoying himself, and that he needed no pity.

All the same, he was obviously glad to see her, and as she stepped down onto the harbour-side he came forward and put his arms round her and kissed her, and then, turning in the direction of the villa, drew her arm through his in a companionable way.

"Hello, darling," he greeted her. "Did you have a good trip? What was it like?"

"Pretty much like here," she said, "but lovely all the same. Have you been working hard?"

"Up to about an hour ago – then I stopped, and I started to feel rather lonely, so I thought I'd wander down here and wait for you." He kissed the top of her head. "You look lovely. I think you're getting a tan, too."

Alec passed them at that moment, and called a cheerful greeting as he strode on ahead. "Off to refill my plastic bag!" he called, waving it.

"What was all that about?" Greig asked when he had gone.

"Oh, he shared his lunch with me," Sarah said lightly.

"I thought you were to be given a packed lunch?"

"We all had one, but he'd brought some extras along, meat and things. The packed lunch was bread and cheese and olives, and he thought it was rather dull, so he brought extra things with him." She waited with trepidation to see how he would take it.

"That was nice of him," Greig said, perfectly naturally and easily. Sarah was so relieved she thought then about telling him the whole story of the photograph, but at the last moment she lost her nerve and thought better of it. "Yes, it was, wasn't it?" she said, making little of it.

"Well, what did you do all afternoon?" Greig asked her. They were walking up the hill now, raising a rich dust. The sun was going down, and the last lizards and gekkos were enjoying what sunshine remained on the hot stones of the little wall that bordered the road. Birds were flying to and fro in the trees with their usual early evening activity, and the swallows were out getting their fill of the insects that gathered at dusk. They darted everywhere,

85

swooping almost under Sarah and Greig's feet, flickering in the shade of the cypress trees, showing their flash of white like tiny ghosts.

"I walked," Sarah said, "and admired the view, and found a little bay all to myself and had a swim, and then lay in the sun and read my book."

"And that's all?" Greig said with a laugh. "You could have done that here, without going on a boat trip. I imagined you'd be sightseeing or something, in with a party. Were you all alone all the time?"

"Yes – but I wanted to be. It was nice. And as for doing the same thing here – well, I could have, of course, but the actual boat trip was lovely, and that was the main part of the afternoon for me."

"Ah well, as long as you enjoyed yourself," Greig said. They passed through a shadowy part of the lane, where the cypresses made a deep black shadow like well-water across the path, and here Greig stopped and drew her to him to kiss her, lightly and tenderly on the lips. He held her away from him a little and looked at her earnestly. "You know that I'm very fond of you, don't you?" he asked her gently. He seemed troubled, and for a moment Sarah wondered if he somehow knew what had worried her. He seemed about to tell her something.

"Of course," she said. "Is there something wrong?"

"No," he said, "nothing wrong." But he pulled her against him and hugged her hard and briefly, as if they were about to be parted for ever and this was their last moment together. Then he let her go and continued up the hill as if nothing had happened. All the same, she shivered as she stepped out of the shadow into the sunlight again, as if a goose had walked over her grave.

"Did you know there's a special do on tonight?" he asked her as they walked on.

"Yes," she said, and was about to add Alec told me, but changed it at the last moment to, "someone on the boat told me."

"But we don't have to go," she added, thinking perhaps that they could eat out somewhere.

"No, that's all right," Greig said, misunderstanding her. "I never meant to work in the evenings as well, not if I got enough done during the day. I wouldn't deprive you of the fun. In any case," he went on as she opened her mouth to tell him she didn't mind, "I'd quite like to go myself. I've been thinking that I ought to mix more with the other guests. I'm a bit of a dull dog when it comes to company. I'd like to change that from now on, and I might as well start here on holiday where it's at least easier to be sociable than at home."

"Well, if you want to go," she said, resigned, and then realised that her tone of voice was not very welcoming to a man coming out of his shell for the first time. She squeezed the arm she held and said affectionately, "It'll be lovely to go to the party with you, darling."

"Well who were you thinking of going with?" he asked, and she realised just in time that it was a joke. A guilty conscience is a most inconvenient thing she thought.

Preparations for the barbecue were already well under way when they arrived at the villa. The side lawn and verandah were being used, and strings of lights, white and coloured, had been hung along the house and in necklaces from the house to the trees. The barbecue was alight and smouldering, and the smell of the burning charcoal overlaid the more familiar perfumes of the night-scented jasmine and stocks, and the lingering daytime scent of roses.

Tables were set up on the verandah, and a bar was in process of being laid out, and already some guests were assembling, mostly those who had not been on the boat trip, with glasses in their hands. One of the villa staff passed them as they went in, bearing an enormous tray of raw kebabs towards the fire, and Sarah said as she passed,

"Are we late?"

"Oh no," said the girl, "there's plenty of time. The fire takes a while to get going. We always allow for the people who are out on the boats anyway. You've plenty of time for a shower, or whatever."

"Is it a dress-up evening?"

"Just as you please," said the girl, smiling. "Only I shouldn't wear anything too smart if you're intending to sit on the grass. But there'll be dancing later on."

The girl passed on, and Sarah turned to Greig. "I think I'll just go and have a shower and get changed. Shall I meet you in the bar, or what?"

"I think I'll get smartened up, too," he said, walking on with her towards their rooms. "Why don't you just tap on my door when you're ready, and we'll go together?"

After her shower, Sarah considered what to wear. She wanted to look good for Greig, but on the other hand she didn't want to look overdressed if everyone else was going to turn up in jeans. In the end she decided on her mulberry-coloured skirt, with the yellow silk blouse that had the big loose sleeves closing in to a tight cuff at the wrist. She drew back the front part of her hair into a knot at the back of her head and let the rest fall loose from underneath it. A trace of lipstick, and a touch of blue shadow to her eyelids was sufficient in the way of make-up, and when she called for Greig she was rewarded for her care by a long, admiring look.

"You should have been a model," he said to her.

"I don't quite know how to take that," she said.

"I mean that you have a knack of making simple clothes look special. And you're always exactly right for the occasion. A very great ability for a person in the public eye."

"So I won't disgrace with you when I have to entertain your famous clients, when you're qualified?" she teased him. An indefinable shadow crossed his face, but was gone in an instant, leaving him only a little more grave than before.

"You would never disgrace me," he said. "We both know that." And a thrill of trepidation passed over her as she wondered, would he still say that after seeing the photograph, the awful, awful photograph? She must find occasion during the evening to speak to the most understanding-looking of the girls about it.

The barbecue was going strong when they reached the verandah, and people were coming and going with loaded plates, while the air was full of the smell of cooking meats. The guests were divided about fifty-fifty on how to dress. Those in jeans or casuals were sitting on the grass or verandah step with their plates, while those in smarter clothes secured tables on the verandah or ate standing up on the lawn. Two chefs in white aprons and caps were tending the fire and turning over the meat with long forks: there were sausages and spare ribs and a variety of kebabs and chops all sizzling away. The villa girls were taking it in turn to help serve both the meat and at the table next to the grill, where were spread bowls of salad ingredients, baskets of bread, cheeses, and fruits.

The bar was serving wine (to be paid for) and soft drinks (free), and they were told that the proper bar would open later if anyone wanted anything stronger. Later, too, in the cleared dining room on the other side of the verandah's french windows, there would be dancing to the villa's disco equipment. As darkness fell the lights were turned on, and grew brighter against the velvety blackness of the sky and the trees, and at once brilliant, many-coloured moths flung themselves in enraptured dance against them, while gekkos scuttled away to shadowed corners. People stood and sat and walked about and talked, the noise grew, a pleasant mixture of conversation and laughter and the satisfied clattering of cutlery and glassware.

Greig and Sarah ate and drank at their table on the verandah and enjoyed the scene, talking to each other a little, now and then, but on the whole silent, just watching. Then Greig got up to replenish their glasses, and on his way back was stopped by Gareth Hunter who got him talking. Sarah, watching, saw him laugh and become animated, and was glad. Then someone else sat down at her table, and got into conversation with Sarah, and when she and Greig drifted together again later they were both in conversations with other guests. They caught each other's eye with complete understanding, smiled, and carried on talking. You see, Sarah addressed him silently, people aren't so bad when you get to know them.

She hardly noticed when the music started up, and in fact was quite surprised when someone came up and asked her if she'd like to dance – she almost said, dance to what? However she looked around for Greig, and seeing him at a little distance and fully engaged in talking to one of the villa's prettier guests and her husband, she smiled and said yes. Greig had never cared much for dancing, so Sarah was doubly pleased when, a little later, he came and claimed her back from her partner, and they did a few circuits of the room in each other's arms in what was more like a leisurely walk than a dance.

"Having a good time?" he asked her.

"Yes. Are you?"

"I'm enjoying myself very much," he said. "It's good to relax after working hard, and everyone here is very pleasant. It's a good group. This holiday certainly wasn't cheap, but I think it's worth it for something so well organised."

"I'm glad you found some pretty girls to talk to," she said teasingly. He bent his head and kissed the tip of her nose.

"They may be pretty, but there's only one beautiful girl here. I'm glad she's having a good time too."

They didn't talk any more after that, but moved in silence, listening to the music, and in complete accord. When the record stopped they parted and smiled at each other, and might have gone on dancing like that for the rest of the night, had they not been interrupted.

"Excuse me, but would you mind if I asked your fiancée for a dance?" Alec asked Greig with perfect politeness, man to man, and without a trace of his usual insolent grin. Greig responded as politely, stepping back and saying,

"Certainly. Thank you, by the way, for looking after her so well on the boat today. I'll see you later, Sarah."

The music started again, and Greig moved off the dance floor, while Alec crooked his arms for her, his face still a polite mask. Sarah stepped just close enough to him to make dancing possible, and as they began to move said crossly,

"I like the way you ask *him* if you can dance with me, but never think of asking *me* if I want to."

"Hush," he murmured, drawing her closer. "You don't want people to think we're quarrelling, do you? People only quarrel if they're very well known to each other."

"Let me go," she hissed, trying to draw back the few inches he had encroached, but his arms, as she already knew, were strong, and she could make no impression on them.

"Relax," he said. "You'll find it much more enjoyable if you relax and let yourself go along with the movement. Besides, you'll look like a duck with your back end stuck out like that."

"If you don't let me go, I'll scream," she whispered violently to him. For answer he drew her even closer, so that her head was on his shoulder and his cheek was against her hair.

"Scream," he murmured, swaying her with the music. The song was 'Till there was You', and he sang the words softly to her as they moved. Finding resistance was no help, Sarah at last relaxed, hoping that he would forget to hold her so tightly if she didn't pull away from him, and that she would be able by degrees to increase the distance between them to a respectable one without his noticing.

After so many years, it was strange to be held this closely by anyone who was not Greig. Greig was very much taller than her, and when he hugged her, her head only came up to his chest. She could only ever cuddle him in bits, she could never get her arms right round him. Alec was much shorter, only a few inches taller than her. His body felt strange, but comfortable as he pressed her close. Her head fitted neatly onto his shoulder, her arms reached his shoulders without any great stretch.

She began to be intensely aware of him, of his hard, muscular chest and arms – she wondered if he played some sport to keep so fit. She remembered how he had looked in his bathing trunks, and the power of his bare shoulders, and she shivered suddenly, and he held her even closer. The pleasant smell of his skin was in her nostrils – disconcertingly unlike Greig's, for Greig always smelled of his after-shave, but Alec used none. Sarah could feel the heat of his cheek against her head, was terribly aware of their hands linked together, of his soft rapid breathing so close beside her.

The record was a long one, but she longed for it never to end. Their bodies swayed in complete accord; Alec's hand slid under her hair and touched the back of her neck, and she trembled. She turned her head a little and their cheeks touched, and the longing swept over her to kiss him and be kissed by him, a wild, dizzy, mad longing to drown in sweet kisses.

Madness indeed, as she realised moments later when the music stopped and she drew back from him, dazed at the feelings that had swept through her. Madness, absolute madness! She hardly knew the man, she was engaged to be married, she was Greig's fiancée – to be thinking these thoughts about a complete stranger! She couldn't even plead the excuse of the wine, because as she freed herself from Alec's arms, she knew she was stone cold sober. She hardly dared meet his eyes, afraid of the feelings she might read there, and the feelings they might reawaken in her; but when she did, his dark eyes were serious, and perfectly friendly, the eyes of a person she had known all her life, and trusted.

"Thank you for the dance," she said. "And now I must go and find Greig."

"Dance again," he asked her softly, but he didn't try to hold her back when she broke away from him. She went out onto the verandah to find Greig, but she couldn't see him anyway, and afraid that Alec might follow her out, she almost ran to the next door and went into the villa through the entrance hall, with the vague idea of looking for Greig in his room. Looking back over her shoulder to see if she was being followed, she was not looking where she was going, and she bumped into someone coming out of the inner door of the dining room. With a small scream, she saw it was Alec.

"Steady!" he admonished her, grinning. "Throwing yourself into my arms like that – I might get the wrong idea about you."

"Let me go!" she cried, trying to pull away from him,

and finding herself held she struggled and began to cry. "Let me go, let me go!"

As she jerked her head away something pulled her hair, and the sharp pain made her cry out. Seeing her alarm, Alec was concerned, and tried to calm her.

"It's all right, it's all right. Keep still. I'm caught in your hair, juggins, that's all. I can't get free if you don't keep still."

"Let me go," she cried again, and putting up her hand to his shoulder to push him away, the catch of her bracelet got caught too, in his pullover. It was too much for Alec, who began to laugh.

"Trust us!" he said. "I might have known I'd get hopelessly tangled up with you." He continued to laugh, while trying to extricate his arm from behind her, and she jerked again and yelped with pain.

"Look," he said, trying to be reasonable, "you'll have to keep still or it'll get worse. My watch is caught in your hair, and I can't get free. I'll have to use my other hand, or I'll hurt you. But if you don't keep still it'll pull. All right?"

Recovering herself a little, Sarah nodded, cautiously, and remained still. Then she began to think it rather funny herself, and she began to laugh too, silently at first, but then beginning to snigger. "Don't," Alec pleaded. "You'll start me off, and we'll be stuck like this for ever."

"I can't help it, I just thought what we must look like," Sarah said, beginning to be breathless with laughter.

"What a girl! Tears one minute and laughter the next," Alex said, but his attempts to free himself were becoming weaker as his laughter overcame him. They were pressed

95

together face to face, and Sarah's arms were against his shoulders while his were around her. It was a ridiculous position to be in, and she could only giggle weakly. It didn't even sober her when, inevitably, Greig, who had been looking for her, came out through the dining room door and found them. Alec's back was to him, but Sarah saw him at once, and the expression on his face only made her want to laugh the more.

"Oh," Greig said, stopping short with shock. "Don't let me interrupt anything, will you?"

"Who's that? Oh, it's you," Alec said, waltzing Sarah round a degree or two so he could see. "Give us a hand will you, old man?"

"You seem to be managing very well on your own," Greig said stiffly. "May I ask what you're doing with my fiancée?"

"Now, Greig, it isn't what you think," Sarah began.

"I seem to be rather attached here," Alec said, trying to control his laughter.

"So I see," Greig said. "I'm still waiting for an explanation."

"Oh, do stop talking like a bad film, and help us," Sarah implored, still giggling. "Can't you see he's stuck? He's got his watch caught in my hair, and my bracelet's caught in his jumper. Get us out, for heaven's sake."

In silence Greig investigated, and released the catch of Alec's watch from Sarah's under-hair, and as soon as Alec was free and able to step back a pace from Sarah, she was able herself to untangle her bracelet.

"I'm afraid I've snagged it," she said. "It's pulled a

loop out. I'd mend it for you if we were at home, but I've nothing here."

"It's all right, it doesn't matter. I've pulled out quite a hank of your hair, so we're quits."

"When you've finished being noble, perhaps you'd like to tell me what's going on?" Greig said. His nostrils were flaring with suppressed anger, a dangerous sign, Sarah knew from experience.

"Calm down," she told him. "You see for yourself we were tangled up, that's all. It's nothing to get annoyed about."

"I'm perfectly calm," Greig said, "and I could see for myself you were tangled up. I'd just like to know how you *got* into such a position. How long has this been going on?"

"*Nothing*'s going on," Sarah shouted, beginning to lose her temper. Alec was keeping out of it, but there was a little smile on his face that boded no good. "I came out here looking for you, and I wasn't looking where I was going. I bumped into Alec, and he got caught in my hair, and I panicked and got caught in his jumper. That's all."

"That's all?" Greig said in a maddening voice. Sarah was about to yell at him, but she caught sight of Alec's funny expression and controlled herself. "Yes," she said calmly. "That's all."

Greig looked from one of them to the other, puzzled. Alec had asked to dance with her, and a few minutes later he found them alone together in what looked as though it had developed from a passionate clinch. Yet the story was so ridiculous, it had to be true. Sarah saw that he needed to save face.

"I was looking for you to ask for the next dance. Come on, let's go back in." She put her hand on his arm, but he pulled away, not roughly, but firmly.

"No, thank you. I don't want to dance any more. I came to say I was off to bed anyway. It's late enough for me."

"Oh, not yet, Greig!" Sarah pleaded.

"What's the matter? You don't have to go to bed because I do. Don't forget you don't have to get home or anything. You stay and have a good time." Sarah was puzzled now in her turn. Was he being nasty, making himself a martyr, or was he being genuine? It sounded genuine. He didn't seem to be sarcastic, but perfectly reasonable, which, after his jealous outburst a few minutes ago was perfectly *un*reasonable. She didn't know what to think.

"I won't have a good time if you go to bed," she said at last. The pause had been just too long for it to sound natural.

"Don't be silly, Sarah," he said. "Have another dance. I'm sure there are lots of people who'd like to dance with you. Have another dance with Mr. – " He looked vaguely at Alec, as though he didn't really see him. "I'll see you in the morning. How about a swim before breakfast?" And without waiting for an answer he turned and went away in the direction of the cells.

"He's upset," Sarah said bleakly when he had gone.

"Was he? He seemed perfectly reasonable to me. A nice guy."

"That's how I know he's upset. He isn't usually a nice guy," Sarah said unguardedly.

"Well, never mind, let's have another dance."

"No," she said quickly, "I don't want to dance with you again."

"Then let's have another drink, or something more to eat."

"No," she said. "I think I'll go to bed too."

'That won't do any good," Alec said understandingly. "You wouldn't sleep, and anyway, who do you think's going to tell him you didn't stay up after him?"

"I'd tell him myself."

"Don't," he said. "Take my advice and don't. It won't make him feel any better, and it'll make you feel a lot worse."

Sarah looked at him, wondering how much he understood, how much he meant. Then she shrugged.

"Oh well, I might as well have another drink, because you're perfectly right, I wouldn't sleep." They went back out onto the verandah, where the party was still going strong. In between intervals of worrying, she even continued to enjoy herself. But it was obvious now that, whatever else happened, Greig mustn't see the photograph. He'd never believe the same story twice, even if it did happen to be true.

CHAPTER EIGHT

In consequence of a heavy supper and more wine than she was used to; or the conflicting emotions of the evening; or perhaps a mixture of them all, Sarah slept heavily and badly, falling from one nightmare to another and waking very late, unrefreshed, and with a raging thirst.

Groaning she reached for her watch, stared at it without comprehension, and at the same instant heard the breakfast bell ring.

"Oh hell," she said aloud, quite mildly, considering how she was feeling, and dragged herself out of bed. A quick splash of water on the face, and into the first clothes that came to hand. She dragged her hair back and secured it with a rubber band in the way expressly forbidden by all leading crinologists, and rushed out of her room, still frantically blowing her nose, which felt as if it had been involved with a professional boxer.

And she was supposed to have been swimming before breakfast with Greig. Hell again. Double hell. She had been a fool to be tempted into trying that ouzo. She should have known it would do her no good by the smallness of the glasses they served it in. The sun was shining fit to burst and the birds were singing with a noise comparable, in terms of her headache, to fifteen reggae bands, or the fast lane of the M1 in rush-hour. A gekko, sunning himself on the cloister rail, declined to move as she approached and poked his tongue out at her as she hurried past.

"A lot you know about it," she muttered to him irritably, and then wished she'd kept quiet. The dining room was almost full when she arrived, and there was the usual cheerful hum of voices. Greig was sitting at their table already – treble hell! – and reading his newspaper with an air of forbidding calm, while he sipped at his orange juice. Sarah smiled a pallid greeting at one or two people and slipped into her seat opposite Greig with the minimum of fuss. He glanced up but didn't smile.

"Morning," he said. "Sleep well?"

Is he being funny? Sarah wondered. No, she decided, just conventional. "No," she said, or rather, croaked. "Not very well. I kept having nightmares. Too much to eat the night before, I expect."

"Did you stay up very late?" he asked, still looking over his paper calmly.

"Not very. Why?"

"I wondered, that's all. I went for a swim, and I looked in on you to see if you were awake, but you seemed to be sleeping very heavily, so I didn't wake you."

"You'd have done me a favour if you did," she said. "I was having the most awful nightmares about – "

"Don't tell me," he said quickly. "I hate other people's dreams. They make me shiver."

A waiter came to take her order, and she asked for double fruit juice and a large pot of coffee.

"Nothing to eat?" Greig asked, with a look of quiet amusement.

"Don't talk to me of food," she shuddered delicately. "I don't think I ever want to eat anything again in my life."

"And you always had such a good appetite."

"Please change the subject, Did you have a nice swim?"

"I didn't go in the end. Thought I'd wait for you, and go after breakfast instead. I just wandered about and looked at things. Did you take many pictures yesterday?"

"Pictures?" She felt herself turn white.

"Photographs."

The photograph. Recollection came flooding back to her. Quadruple hell, possibly even quintuple hell! It was this morning they would be brought to the villa, possibly were already here. Were they in the vestibule as she came past? She couldn't for the life of her remember – she had not been looking. Was that why he was talking about photographs? Had he already seen it? With an effort she brought her mind back to what he was saying.

"Sorry?"

"I said, I wanted to know how many shots were left on that film. Did you finish yesterday? Because if not I thought I'd take one or two . . ."

So he hadn't already seen it, she thought as he continued to talk. But at any minute – she had to know if they had arrived yet. She couldn't see into the hall from where she sat, and unable to bear it any longer she jumped up and dashed across the dining room to the door. One glance round told her that the vestibule was innocent of any damaging evidence. She stopped short, tried to think of an excuse for having come over here, and slowly,

102

shamefacedly, returned. Her cheeks, that had paled, were red now, and not only Greig stared at her in surprise. She sat down again and applied herself to her coffee.

"Are you all right?" he asked her, sounding quite concerned.

"Yes, I'm fine," she said, not meeting his eyes.

"I thought you were going to be sick," he said. "You went quite white, and then dashing across the room like that – "

That was a good excuse. "I thought I was going to be for a minute, and then I realised I wasn't," she said. "Sorry."

"Perhaps you ought to go and lie down," he suggested. Lie down? If she could get away from Greig, she might be able to hang around the lobby and get the photos first.

"Yes, perhaps I should lie down – " she began.

"I'll just finish my breakfast, and then I'll come and sit with you quietly, reading."

"Oh, there's no need – "

"I wouldn't disturb you, and I don't think you should be alone, in case you are sick," he said firmly. That was no good. She thought hastily.

"Well, perhaps I should get some fresh air," she said. "That would clear my head better than anything. Why don't we go down onto the beach and just relax in the sun?" If she could get him at sufficient distance from the villa, she could invent some excuse to leave him there and come back – something vital left in her room, or something like that.

"I don't know that bright sunshine would be the best

103

thing for you if you've got a headache," Greig said doubtfully.

"Oh, my head's all right," she said hastily. "It's just that I've got a stuffy nose. Some fresh air – fresh sea air – would do the trick. In fact, I think we should go straight out now." She wanted to get him away from the vestibule as soon as possible, before the man turned up.

"Right now?" Greig sounded surprised, as well he might, at her sudden change of ideas. "Well, all right, if you think it would do you good. But I think you ought to have your sunhat and sunglasses, if you have got a headache. Are you sure you don't feel sick still?"

"No, I don't feel sick at all," she said truthfully. "I just feel in need of some fresh air."

"All right then, darling," he said obligingly. He finished his toast and coffee, while Sarah, on tenterhooks, gulped at her orange juice and stared around the room restlessly. "I notice your partner of last night isn't here this morning," Greig said pleasantly, making conversation. "Looks like a clear case of the morning after."

All the better, Sarah thought. The less I see of him, the better – he seems to make trouble for me every time I bump into him. I wonder what time the man will come. I would have thought he'd come early, since everyone starts the day at dawn around these parts. They have to, I suppose, if they're going to sleep a large part of the afternoon. I'll have to try and find out – shake Greig off somehow, just for a minute or two.

"Let's go, huh?" she said, pushing back her chair. Greig gave her a look of amusement.

"You're in a hurry to get out there," he said. "All

104

right, I'll come." And resignedly leaving his toast he stood up and followed her towards the door. As she approached it, however, she heard voices in the hall outside – a man's voice, sounding like an Englishman, one of the villa's staff perhaps, speaking Greek haltingly, and then a high, piping, old man's voice, also speaking Greek and laughing shrilly. Realisation hit her violently – the high piping voice belonged to the photographer: he had brought the photographs and was at that very instant setting them up in the vestibule!

She stopped short, so suddenly that Greig almost ran into her.

"What's up?" he asked, sounding slightly annoyed. She turned and stared wildly at him, her mouth open, trying to think of something to say. He looked at her with a mixture of exasperation and concern. "Really, Sarah, I do think you're acting peculiarly this morning – "

"Not this way," she said hoarsely. "Let's go out through the french windows."

"But we're here now. Are you sure you feel all right? You look as if you're having a stroke or something."

"Go out through the other door," she commanded him, pushing ineffectually at his chest and making no impression.

"You're not that desperate for fresh air," he said, taking her arm and guiding her towards the door into the lobby. "Anyway it's quicker this way. I think you ought to go and lie down, really I do. Have a sleep and get up later, when you're feeling a bit better."

Talking thus he guided her irresistibly into the hall. Her feet moved on their own – she had no control over them, not even when she saw, as she had known she would see, the little old man standing talking to a couple of members of staff in front of a large board he had just erected opposite the reception desk; and on the board were pinned, unmistakeably, the photographs. Her doomed footsteps took her on across the hall with Greig talking kindly in her ear – and, to her astonishment, straight past the noticeboard and out into the sunshine! He had not even given the pictures a glance. Her knees went wobbly with relief, and he had to catch hold of her and help her down the steps.

"My darling, you *aren't* well," he said, but Sarah turned and flung herself into his arms with gratitude.

"You are nice," she said. "And I'm all right, really – or I will be when I get down to the beach. Lack of oxygen, that's all it was." No problem now. Just get down to the sand, and at some time later make an excuse to pop up, buy the photo, and destroy it. And Bob's your uncle. She smiled at Greig so nicely that he was reassured, and they turned and were about to walk towards the cliff steps when Alec Russell came out of the villa and called a cheerful hello to them.

"Have you seen the photographs?" he asked with an innocent smile. Sarah's jaw dropped, and then she gave him the most ferocious snarl from behind Greig's shoulder.

"What photographs are those?" Greig asked politely, but without interest.

"The ones taken on the trip yesterday. There was a professional chap taking snaps of everybody, and he's brought them along for people to order. Didn't you see them? They're in the hall here."

106

"No, I didn't – I must have walked past them," Greig said, starting back up the steps towards Alec. "You didn't tell me about those, Sarah."

Sarah simply couldn't believe it. She couldn't believe that Alec would do anything so cruel and stupid, and she stared at him with a mixture of astonishment and fury, but he only smiled at Greig and pretended to ignore her looks.

"There wasn't one of me," she said in a last ditch attempt, "so I didn't think to mention it. He was asking if we wanted our pictures taken, but I didn't." And she followed them in as she spoke, knowing that there would be no bluffing this one away. And yet, what could Alec be about, to bring Greig's attention to it in this way? She followed Greig's tall, elegant back towards the notice-board and waited for the explosion, but it didn't come. Like someone slowly taking their fingers out of their ears when a banger hasn't gone off, she went up beside him and looked too, her eyes going at once to the empty place where photograph number ten had been, and was no longer.

Greig looked over the pictures with as much attention as they merited, and then said,

'Pity there wasn't one of you, Sarah. They're rather nice. Shall we go? We were just going down to the beach," he added in explanation to Alec. "Excuse us, won't you?"

"Of course," Alec said, and stood aside for them to pass. Sarah caught his eye, and he smiled at her complaisantly, while she gave him a look of utter fury.

"Smile, you're on Candid Camera," he murmured as

107

she passed, and she hung back for the fraction of a second it was necessary to hiss at him with venom,

"I hate practical jokers!"

Knowing, however, that at least he did not intend to give the show away, Sarah could forgive the desire to embarrass her, and put the whole episode out of her head for the rest of the morning. She and Greig had a bathe and sat on the beach talking for a while, and since Sarah assured him she felt perfectly all right again, he readily agreed to her plan of walking in the opposite direction to the villa, over the rise into the next bay.

"There's a village there, too, so perhaps we could have a bite of lunch together before you have to come back," she added.

"I think I might take this afternoon off from the work, actually," Greig said casually. "It's gone so well up to now that I think a day off will do me more good than harm. And besides, it's a long time since we had a serious talk together."

"What about?"

"About anything. We aren't often alone together with the leisure to talk things out. We ought to take the opportunity while we're on holiday just to be together."

"It all sounds very serious," Sarah said, wondering what was on his mind. He smiled down at her and squeezed her hand.

"No need to be serious yet," he said, and left it at that.

He stood up and offered her his hand to pull her to her feet. She felt vaguely threatened by what he had said, and yet he was as pleasant as could be, not as if anything bad was on his mind. "I should go back to the villa and get tidied up," she said.

"You look fine. Just as you are."

"But we should collect things – "

"There's nothing we need."

"Money?"

He patted his pocket. "I've plenty. Come on." He took her hand and strode off down the beach, almost as if he were saying, come on, let's live a little. This was not the Greig she knew, who would hardly stir from his own fireside to answer the front door without putting on a jacket and tie. There was some indefinable difference coming over him. Could it be the magic of the island working on him? Whatever it was, it seemed that she was going to find out during the course of the afternoon she was to spend alone with him.

The walk over the hill in the fresh air made her feel much better, and when they arrived in the next village, Sarah mentioned that she felt rather hungry.

"I couldn't face breakfast when I woke up, but now I could do murder to a piece of toast," she said.

"That'll teach you to stuff yourself at barbecues," Greig said, smilingly.

"It wasn't the food – it was the ouzo that did it," Sarah confessed. "I knew at the time I'd regret it, but I still went ahead and tried it. You know how it is – someone persuades you – "

"The woman tempted me, and I did eat," Greig quoted. "Or in your case, the serpent. Who was it?"

"Alec Russell," Sarah admitted reluctantly. How that name did come up.

"I'll knock his block off," Greig said, but as pleasantly as possible. Certainly the air seemed to be agreeing with him. "Well, shall we stop at one of these cafes and get something for you to eat?"

"Oh, yes please. What about that one over there?"

"Trust you to pick out the tattiest one," Greig said, but he changed direction at once.

"I don't think it's tatty – it's just small and old." They chose places at the wooden refectory table which were in the shade but facing the best view, and when the proprietor came out to them, ordered coffee, and bread and fruit for Sarah.

"You'll spoil your lunch, but what does it matter," Greig said. He leaned back in his chair, narrowing his eyes against the sun, and looking the epitome of relaxation. Sarah marvelled at him.

"You must be feeling pretty good," she said. "Your work has gone well, has it?"

Greig did not even move his eyes. A sparrow flew down from the roof and landed near them, made an enquiring cheep, and hopped a pace nearer.

"I'm not even thinking about my work. A twenty-four-hour amnesty."

"Well, that's nice to hear. A bit of a change of attitude, isn't it?" Sarah asked. She too was watching the sparrow, who hopped hesitantly forward towards their feet, and stopped again to put his head on one side and challenge them.

"I've been doing quite a bit of thinking over the past couple of days," Greig said, and then paused, as if he were not sure whether to tell her the results of that thinking or not. The cafe owner came out with a wooden tray bearing their order, and the sparrow hopped two forward and one to the side, like a chess knight, its eye on the tray and with no fear of the proprietor at all. "Thank you," Greig said, and as the man went away, he picked up the coffee pot and began to pour. Sarah reached over a hand and dug a small piece out of the crust of bread and threw it down, and the sparrow pounced on it, its faith in humanity fully justified. "I've been coming to the conclusion that my attitudes to a number of things have been perhaps mistaken in the past," Greig went on.

"Oh, really? Like what?" A second sparrow flew down and hopped forward eagerly. The first squeaked indignantly, as well as it could through a moustache and beard of fresh Greek bread, and turned its back on the newcomer.

"Haven't you any idea?" Greig asked. "Isn't there anything you think I ought to have rethought in the past?"

The second sparrow hopped round the first, trying to keep that mouthful of bread in sight as the first sparrow turned on the spot. They made a good excuse for Sarah and Greig not to look at each other.

"Well," she said hesitantly, "I don't want to bring up old quarrels – "

"Nor do I," Greig said quickly, "but I've sometimes reacted to things in a certain way, and I've been trying to work out for myself why. And I came to the con-clusion – "

A shadow fell across the pavement, and both sparrows flew away with a chirp of alarm. Sarah and Greig looked up, and saw Alec Russell standing before them, smiling a cheerful greeting.

"Hullo! I saw you from across the street – thought it was you. May I join you?"

"Well, actually," Sarah was beginning, realising that she and Greig had been on the point of a serious private talk, but to her surprise Greig half stood with friendly politeness and said,

"Certainly – do! We were just having a little brunch. Sarah couldn't face breakfast."

Sarah saw Alec minutely adjusting to the unexpected cordiality of the meeting as he sat down. "You'll spoil your lunch," he said pleasantly to Sarah, and glanced at his watch, "for which it is almost time."

"No, no, you've got it wrong," she said. "I'm not spoiling my lunch by a late breakfast, I'm actually not-spoiling my dinner, by an early lunch."

"Eh?" he pretended to be bamboozled. Greig laughed.

"That's a good one. And it's a good idea, actually. I think I'll join you in something now, and then when we get back to the hotel, we'll have a good appetite for dinner."

"Oh well," Alec shrugged, "I might as well go along with the general trend." And when the cafe owner came out, he ordered himself a salad and coffee, and Greig asked for more bread, and some cheese.

"I had a look at a paper this morning," Alec said when their orders were in front of them. "I see the bank rate's coming down again."

"About time too," Greig said, and the two of them plunged into a discussion of economics, a topic of conversation on which Sarah had no information and less

112

interest. She let her attention wander away as she applied herself to her coffee and bread, and she amused herself by feeding the sparrows, who flew down again as soon as Alec was settled in his seat. Though she didn't listen to what they were saying, she listened to the tone of their conversation, and was glad, for no particular reason, that they seemed this morning to be so friendly. It was a strange thing about men, she thought, that as soon as they could retreat into some 'male' province, like economics or football, they became firm friends.

It all began, of course, in childhood, when gangs of little boys got together and said 'Don't let's tell the girls – they spoil everything', and trotted off to the gang hut to be important together. Adult little boys had men's clubs, and even the most civilised of men had 'male' topics of conversation about which they could say "Women don't understand." It wasn't of course that women were incapable of understanding – it was that the subjects themselves were so dull, no-one would want to understand. They chose dull subjects on purpose, of course, to keep women out. Sarah smiled at her own thoughts at that point, and both the men looked at her with interest.

"You were going to say something?" Greig asked.

"A penny for them?" Alec offered.

"I think that's a loathsome expression," Sarah said to the latter.

"Doesn't take account of inflation, I grant you," he replied, shooting a glance at Greig.

"Nor the drop in the bank rate," he agreed. Sarah looked from one to the other.

113

"You two seem to be very cock-a-hoop. Quite like old friends."

"We read the same paper," Alec said, quick to find something to say that would avoid embarrassment. "That makes us almost blood-brothers."

This seemed strange to Sarah at least. She could not fathom the minds of men. Yesterday Greig seemed ready to tear Alec apart, and today they were like two members of the same gang. Still, it was better than warfare, she supposed.

"What are we going to do after lunch, or brunch, or whatever it is we're eating?" she asked Greig.

"I don't know. What do you want to do?"

"I'd like to look around the shops first," she said. "I haven't had a chance yet in any of the places we've been."

"*You*'ve been," Greig corrected her. "All right, if that's what you want. But it won't take us very long. What would you like to do for the rest of the afternoon?"

"Don't plan on rushing me through the shops and out the other side," Sarah warned. "I want to explore all the back streets and find the fantastic bargains people always come across in stories. I'm sure there are some lovely little shops down the alleys."

"There are," Alec said. "I've been over this village fairly thoroughly, so I can act as your guide – for a consideration of course."

"I might buy you a drink tonight," Greig said generously, "but that's as far as that goes."

"Done," Alec said. Sarah was not sure how she felt about this threesome business, but there were two against

114

one, and if that was what they wanted, she had little option but to go along with it. But she wished she knew what it was that Greig was about to say when Alec interrupted their tete-a-tete.

CHAPTER NINE

Looking back on it afterwards, Sarah always thought that afternoon had a strange, dreamlike quality that set it apart from reality. It was not only that Greece was an enchanted place, in which everything seemed to happen on a plane above the normal, but there was something about that particular time, and the three of them being together. The grouping shifted and changed all the time. Sometimes it would be as if she and Alec were children running wild, being followed by an indulgent parent in Greig; at other times, she and Greig would seem like a married couple entertaining a younger, unmarried brother; and other times again, the strangest to Sarah, the two men would seem to be ranged together in protecting her and pampering her and seeing that she enjoyed herself and didn't get hurt. At those times it seemed that they had some shared secret together, from which she was, regretfully, excluded.

Alec took upon himself the role of guide around the village, and it did seem that he knew the place, for he led her as if by instinct to the very places she wanted to go. He found little shops in crooked back streets, where she was dazzled with displays of leather sandals and embroidered caftans, woven rugs and ponchos, shoulder bags, sheepskins, scarves and belts. At another shop were shelves of lovely pottery, china and stoneware, and wooden kitchen implements, bowls and boxes, beautifully made and simply designed. At another again was jewellery, astonishingly cheap, sometimes amusing, sometimes beautiful. She was even interested in the food shops, the cheeses and cooked meats and the wonderful assortment of fruit and vegetables.

Yet oddly enough she had no compulsion to go mad and spend, as she might have expected of herself. She was content, on the strange, dreamy afternoon, to look and handle and admire, and to have the two men point out to her the things they thought she would like best. It was left to them to make the purchases: the only thing she bought for herself was an olive-wood rolling pin. It was an odd thing for her to buy, considering she lived at home with her mother, who already had one, and never did any cooking herself.

"Why do you want it?" Greig asked her with a curiosity that seemed to conceal unasked questions.

"I don't know," she said, genuinely puzzled. She ran her hands over the smooth, dark-golden length of it. It was all-of-a-piece, the knobs at either end turned gracefully out of the single original block of wood. "It's just so beautiful. I don't suppose I'll ever use it – I just want it."

"Well, I expect you'll have a kitchen of your own one day, and then it will come in useful," Alec said, and she let it go, but she knew that was not why she wanted it.

She expressed as much admiration of the goods as even

the proudest workman could have required of her, but when they saw she had no inclination to buy, the two men bought for her, giving her presents which afterwards brought back to her the enchantment of the island. Greig bought her an over-tunic of white linen so fine it was almost transparent, with an embroidery of white silken threads on the front; and at another shop, a small white china vase with a delft-blue decoration around it of sea-horses and tritons and strange fish.

Alec, though as eager as a terrier in hunting through shops, and though presenting every few minutes some good or other for admiration with a cry of "Look at this!", often proposed buying, but did not actually buy until he found the thing he felt just right. This was in the shop of a jeweller and silver-smith, a shop in which Sarah would have spent more time than all the others, since she loved anything silver. There they found a ring in the shape of a dolphin leaping. When you put it on, his tail was curled round your finger with its flanges resting beside his friendly, bottle-nosed, blunt head. There was something comforting in the curl of his body, something enchanting about his friendly, humorous face – the silversmith had caught exactly the charm of real dolphins in this piece of work. By a stroke of luck that Sarah did not at the time find at all surprising, the ring fitted her exactly, and Alec bought it at once and she did not take it off but wore it out from the shop.

Out again in the sunshine, they wandered in companionable silence up the street and came out into a small square at the top of the village, and there they stopped to discuss what they would do next.

"How about going back for our togs, and having a swim on some deserted beach or other?" Alec suggested. "There are loads of them along this part of the coast."

"I don't feel like going all the way back and then back here again," Greig said. "We should have thought of bringing them with us this morning."

"No use saying that now," Sarah said. "I agree – I don't want to walk all that way back for that. What can we do here?"

"We could go down to the harbour and see if there are any boat trips," Greig said. "Or maybe hire a boat for ourselves and just fool about on the water."

They turned and looked back down towards the sparkling, inviting sea. The kind of indolence was over them which deplored any unnecessary effort, and it seemed unnecessary effort to retrace their steps in however good a cause. They were standing there still, gently arguing, when a small boy ran up to them and with an incomprehensible gabble, invited them by gestures to go with him. He was a slender small boy like a faun, dark curly hair and dark eyes and bare feet like the goat-boy Sarah had seen on the other side of the island, and taking a liking to him she began at once to follow.

"Hey, wait a minute," Greig said. "We don't know what he wants or where he's going."

"It's all right," Sarah said from no more than a conviction that it was, and then remembered. "But you can speak Greek," she said to Alec. "Why don't you ask him."

"How do you know he can?" Greig asked her. On this afternoon she could not be embarrassed by the memory of how she knew. "I heard him," she said only. She had heard him, of course, bargaining with the photographer in the hall at the villa.

"I speak a bit," Alec said. "Enough to get around. I couldn't catch a word the kid said, though – too quick."

"Oh come on," Sarah said impatiently. "What do you think he's doing – leading us into an ambush?"

"It has been known," Greig said, but he followed her anyway. The boy ran ahead of them and led them round a corner where a large stout man with drooping moustaches was standing, obviously waiting for them. The child ran up to him and spoke in Greek, and pointed at the three of them. The man patted the child's head and then turned to them smiling.

"You English?" he said, but didn't wait for an answer. "I am Andreas. I speak English very good. I learn in navy in war. You from the villa? On holiday?"

"Yes," Alec answered for them all. The man nodded.

"I think so, so I send boy. You like to go for ride, on donkeys, up hills to see old church, very fine old ruins? All the way on donkeys, no walking. Take very fine pictures." And he made a dumb-show of taking photographs. Sarah smiled – they had no camera. The two men looked at each other and then at her, seeking opinion. She had no doubts. They had not wanted to exert themselves, and here was something decided for them, something to do thrown in their way without any effort involved.

"I want to go," she said at once.

"How much?" Alec asked, to the point. Andreas spread his hands, and his eyes took on a gleam. This was the part of the business he liked best. He threw himself into the bargaining battle with a will. Alec negotiated for the

English, but after the first exchange carried on in Greek, to show Andreas that he knew what was what. Greig and Sarah listened with amused incomprehension and at last were told by a triumphant Alec that they would be taken to the ruins and back for ten drachma each. He seemed proud of his achievement, but as the old man looked equally self-satisfied, Sarah guessed that ten drachma was exactly the sum both parties had fixed on as right before the argument began.

"But where is it we're going?" Greig asked Alec as the man disappeared down an alley beside his house, presumably to fetch the donkeys.

"A ruined monastery up in the hills. I don't know much about it. I've heard of it – Gareth back at the villa mentioned it as worth a visit, but any more than that I don't know."

"It doesn't matter," said Sarah. "It will make a nice afternoon's trip."

"But I can't ride," Greig objected.

"Anyone can ride a donkey," Alec said. "You just sit on and if it slows up you kick it. In any case, they'll follow the one in front, like elephants. You don't need any skill."

"Greig's worried about looking undignified, aren't you?" Sarah teased.

"Not at all," he denied it. "I'm just glad I wore jeans today. Imagine if I had my good trousers on."

"I'm glad I'm wearing trousers and not shorts," Sarah said. "The leathers pinch your legs if they're bare."

At that moment the small boy appeared leading two chocolate-brown donkeys, and behind him came an even smaller boy, leading two more, a gingery-coloured one, and a small, mouse-grey one. Behind them came the old man, lugging an enormous block of wood whose purpose none of the three could begin to imagine. The boys led the donkeys up to the party, and Greig at once exclaimed,

"They're tiny! They won't be able to carry us!"

"Just count them," Alec said, "and look at the size of the old man. He evidently intends to ride one. That ginger beast looks biggish – perhaps you could have that one."

"It'd never get up the mountain," Greig said, laughing.

"They can carry enormous weights," Alec assured him.

"Thanks," he said ironically. Two pi-dogs came running out after the man, ran round the strangers sniffing and wagging their bushy tails, and then trotted off ceremoniously to wet the gatepost. They had smiling faces and bushy ruffs, and seemed disposed to enjoy everything.

Andreas meanwhile had dragged the wooden block into position, and, apparently satisfied with it, beckoned to Sarah. Visions of beheading floated before her, but she realised at that moment that it was a mounting-block, and that it had been dragged out for her specific use. She had been fondling the velvety muzzle of the little grey donkey, liking his authentically sad and bowed look, and now she pointed at him and said to Andreas,

"Can I have this one?"

"Sure, sure. Very fine little fellow," Andreas said at once. Since it was by far the smallest, she would probably have been given it anyway, but she was glad all the same. To her, donkeys should always be grey to be the genuine article. She could have thrown her leg over it as easily as getting on a bicycle, but she could hardly refuse the offered help since he had gone to all the trouble of bringing out the block – it had suffused his face to a deeper shade of red, and had brought him out in a mild sweat.

So she walked with dignity to the block, mounted it, and allowed herself to be helped with great ceremony onto the narrow back of the little grey donkey.

"Hold on here," Andreas was instructing her, "hold these tight, don't worry, you not fall off." She submitted to that too, for there was no purpose in telling him she had been riding since the age of twelve. The donkey was so narrow and so little that her feet were only about six inches above the ground. She looked down at the dark cross-of-Jesus on his withers, and patted his neck happily, and he shifted his weight from one side to the other and sighed as donkeys do.

Greig had been helped up onto one of the brown donkeys – Andreas was evidently keeping the big ginger jack to cope with his own considerable bulk – and was looking as unsafe as he felt uncomfortable. Alec waved away the offer of help, and standing back a little, made a short run and leap. He reached the donkey's back and went straight over and off the other side. Sarah burst out laughing, realising he was giving them a circus and, by his fooling, trying to make Greig feel happier. It was a piece of kindness that raised him Sarah's estimation. The dogs rushed at him barking madly, and the children shrieked with merriment. Alec stood up, looked bewildered, brushed himself off, and shook his fist at the donkey in dumb show. The donkey flicked its ears against the flies, but made no sign of even noticing him.

123

For five minutes Alec entertained them, pretending that the immobile creature was making it impossible for him to mount, or, having mounted, to remain in the saddle for more than a second. Andreas, seeing that he was to be amused, leaned against his garden gate and chuckled in appreciation while he rolled himself a cigarette. The two little boys made a most satisfactory audience, shrieking with laughter, clutching hold of each other and doubling up, stamping their feet and calling out encouragement. Sarah and Greig were helpless with laughter, the latter having already forgotten his embarrassment at making a public spectacle of himself, and the dogs raced around, barking in a perplexed way at Alec and the donkey impartially.

At last, having almost slipped off sideways, Alec slowly hauled himself upright, grasped the reins, and nodded in a satisfied way at the rest of the party, and seeing the show was over, Andreas shoved himself off the gatepost, lit his cigarette, and rolled over to his own donkey which he mounted slowly from the block. They set off in procession, Andreas leading the way with Greig's donkey following closely, then Alec, and Sarah in the rear. The two dogs were joined by two more, and they ran around the caravan, sometimes in front, sometimes behind, sniffing into everything and grinning up at the riders like the friendly creatures they were. The older of the two children came too, but on foot, springing from rock to rock where the path narrowed, and running on ahead to keep out of the dust.

At first Sarah kept her eyes on Greig, worried about him, for she knew how much he valued his dignity, and how little he could bear looking silly. At home, he was the kind of person who cannot wear a paper hat at Christmas, or join in community singing, or play parlour games that involve making a fool of oneself. She was surprised that he had consented to go on this trip, for riding a donkey was calculated to make him feel awkward. Yet he did not look silly at all – he was young and good looking, and casually dressed in jeans and a shirt, and he looked quite natural astride the little beast and in fact – she found herself thinking – very attractive. She wished she could tell him, but the path was narrow and it was impossible to catch him up to speak to him. However after the first few minutes she saw from his attitude that he had relaxed and was beginning to look round and enjoy himself, and so she stopped worrying about him.

Alec, by complete contrast to Greig, was a person with no worries at all about his public image. He could join in any community action, with such freedom from embarrassment that he did not look at all foolish. He could even make himself look deliberately silly, as he had done for Greig's sake when mounting the donkey, without any material loss of face. He was one of nature's clowns, and though his sense of humour had given her some bad moments, she knew there was no malice in him. He was not good-looking, nor even tall – certainly not impressive, with his smallish, wiry body and reddish hair, but he looked good on a donkey too, as if he had made himself one with his mount and was in complete control.

The ride up into the hills took about forty minutes. They passed quite a number of people, some working in the fields, some standing at the doors of their remote houses, some tending flocks of sheep or goats. All of them waved and smiled, giving the strangers their friendly greeting "Chairete!" and addressing a few words to Andreas. Under the blue, perfect sky, the scene was dreamlike and beautiful, and when after a while Andreas began to sing in a husky but surprisingly tuneful voice, it only added to the dreaminess of the afternoon.

The ruins, when they reached them, were worth seeing. There was an engraved iron plaque on one wall with the bare details in Greek and English, giving the dates of the monastery and a brief history. It had been a ruin since the late nineteenth century when it was destroyed by fire and had never been rebuilt. Andreas, having helped them dismount, took his donkeys to a shady place and himself sat down by them on a piece of broken wall and began to make another roll-up. The little boy searched out bracken fronds to tuck into each donkey's crownpiece to keep the flies off their faces, and then sat down a little way from his father and chewed grass.

The three of them explored the ruins together until Sarah took it into her head to climb the remains of the tower so as to get the view from the top. She had a feeling that Greig would try to stop her if he knew, so she slipped away from them at a moment when they were arguing about the probable age of a certain piece of stonework and went around to the other side to find a convenient place to climb. The inside of the tower must have been wooden, for there was no trace of how the monks had originally climbed up to it, but the outside wall, though sheer, looked easy enough to climb, there being a lot of missing stones, and various jutting ledges and other projections. Sarah was nimble, and feeling each foothold carefully before putting her weight on it, she went up the side of the tower easily, and reached the narrow parapet at the top which was her goal.

The view was marvellous. The monastery was built at the top of the gentle folds of hills that made up the island, and from the vantage point of the tower, she could not only see back the way they had come, right down into the village, but looking the other way she could see the sea on that side too. The whole island was spread out below her in minute and perfect detail, and the air was so clear she could see for immense distances. The hills were soft and rounded, like the billows in a green bedspread suddenly solidified. Over them were scattered the small clumps of cypresses and the olive-groves and the birchwoods. Patches of purple heather and dark, almost black, myrtle varied the texture and colour of the open spaces, and here and there were little white houses and tiny figures of people and animals moving about their daily business.

And round it all in a great azure circle was the sea, merging finally into the equally blue sky, so that she felt as if she were suspended in the very centre of a drop of blue glass, like one of those little pieces of coral set into the middle of a glass paperweight. She was enchanted. Looking down she saw the two men looking up at her, their bodies foreshortened by the height and their faces turned whitely up. They had been looking for her, of course. She waved and shouted down to them,

"I can see right round the island – right to the other side!"

Perhaps because of the waving, or the drawing in her breath to shout, she suddenly wavered, losing her balance, and had to grab at a piece of masonry. It crumbled at her touch, and the firmer stone she took hold of underneath was loose, and wobbled. She realised then how high up she was, how narrow the ledge on which she was standing, how foolish she was to have trusted her weight to a ruin which every stone on the ground proclaimed to be in the process of falling down.

"Oh," she said aloud, and her voiced emerged small and inadequate. She felt like saying 'help,' but at the same time she realised how totally inadequate that would be, since there was no-one near enough to help her, even if they had heard.

"You got yourself up here," she told herself severely, "so you can jolly well get yourself down." That was all very well, but while her mind was functioning normally, and was aware that she was perfectly capable of climbing down what she had just climbed up, her body seemed to have got into a kind of panic all its own, and would not answer her commands. Her hands clutched the loose, crumbling stones, her feet were rigid on the narrow ledge, and her body bent at a ridiculous angle inwards from the edge of the tower. This is silly, she thought, but she couldn't move. I'll have to stay up here for ever, she thought next. Greig will be terrified, poor soul. He can't bear heights, and he doesn't even like to see someone else up high. He'll be in the very worst predicament – afraid for me, but unable to help. He'll stand at the bottom of the tower, unable to tear his eyes away, in an agony of fear, until I finally get cramp and fall. He'll never get over it – he'll be a wreck for the rest of his life, like those train drivers when suicides throw themselves under their trains. Most unfair. But I suppose there's no way you can commit suicide without inconveniencing somebody.

Her thoughts rattled on conversationally in her head, while her body grew more rigid. She could feel the rough cement cutting into her hands as she gripped tighter and tighter. It was a most peculiar situation to be in, like being two different people, her mind seeming quite normal while her body was completely out of control. After a minute or two she forgot Greig, as she had already forgotten Alec, and she clung to the top of the tower, talking to herself inside her head of trains and buses and suicides. She did not know it, of course, but it was a form of hysteria, and her mind was turning away from the knowledge that it was only a matter of time before she fell to her death on the stones below.

CHAPTER TEN

Greig and Alec, who had been wandering about the ruins looking for her, spotted her simultaneously. Greig's natural fear of heights expressed itself at once in anger.

"What the hell is she doing up there?" he exploded, and was opening his mouth to yell at her, when Alec grabbed his arm urgently.

"Don't shout – you'll distract her!" he cried. Greig shut his mouth, but a real and reasoned fear came to replace his first thoughtless anger. He saw then that she was in danger, in the first place that she might slip or over-balance and fall, and in the second place that the tower might give way under her, throwing her down under several tons of stones. His face went white. At that moment Sarah looked down and saw them. They saw her wave, heard her shout something, though the words did not reach them, and then Alec's hand, still on Greig's arm, tightened as they both saw her sway dangerously and grab at the top of the tower behind her. A stone loosened and fell inwards, and they heard it crashing and rattling its way down inside. For a breathless, terrible moment, they waited for the rest of the tower to sink magnificently and fall in on itself; then their breath let out in a hiss as the tower stood firm, with Sarah almost doubled up at the top of it.

As the silence settled again, they waited for her to make a move, but minutes passed and she remained motionless in her uncomfortable pose on the narrow ledge.

"She can't move," Greig said at last.

"Sarah! Come on down!" Alec called to her. "It's all right now – come down!"

"She can't hear you," Greig sid.

"She's frozen," Alec said. "It gets people like that sometimes – they seize up."

"She'll fall. Oh God. She'll fall."

"One of us will have to go up for her," Alec said. Greig only continued to stare upwards at his fiancée, fear written all over his face.

"How will I ever tell her parents," he muttered. Alec felt impatience sweeping over him.

"It's no use standing there planning the funeral," he said harshly. "We've got to do something." Greig looked at him in shock, and then with a great effort he pulled himself together, and with a greater effort admitted the terrible truth.

"I can't go up there. I'm terrified of heights."

For a second Alec felt only impatient scorn for the other man, but it was superseded at once by an unwilling sympathy. He realised how much worse it must make it for Greig, to be prevented from helping his chosen woman by his own miserable fear; and he realised also what a lot it must take to admit of that fear to another man. But there was no time to be wasted in pity. Briskly Alec answered,

131

"Well I'll go up then. It's probably better – I should think I'm lighter than you."

"What can I do?" Greig asked miserably.

"Nothing," Alec said shortly, and looked about for his first handhold. With Greig watching from below, Alec made his way up the sheer tower side, not quite as Sarah had before him, for she had only pleasure in mind. It was an easy climb upwards, but he could not imagine how he was going to get her down the same way. He reached the ledge and climbed onto it at a little distance from Sarah, for he had not wanted to startle her into a sudden move, but as he shuffled towards her cautiously he realised that she was not aware of him. Bent almost double, and clutching the stone parapet so hard her knuckles were white, she was staring ahead of her with glazed eyes.

"Sarah, Sarah, it's me, Alec," he said gently, trying to catch her eye. "It's all right now, I've come to get you down. You can relax now."

She paid him no heed at first, but at last he succeeded in drawing her gaze towards him, and he saw recognition dawn in her eyes.

"Hello, Alec," she said conversationally. "It's a lovely day, isn't it? And a lovely view from here. You can see all over the island. They ought to build a revolving restaurant up here, like the one in the Post Office tower. Have you ever been in it? It's got a lovely view, not so nice as this one of course, but you can see for miles."

She prattled on, her easy tone of voice making the weirdest contrast to her rigid body and staring eyes, and he realised that she was hysterical.

"Calm down, Sarah – it's all right," he said. He put

his hand over hers and tried to prise her fingers loose, but it was beyond him. She had begun to repeat herself, and he was afraid of her tiring too much to make the return climb.

"Desperate situations call for desperate remedies," he said. "Forgive me, Sarah." And gripping her shoulder hard with his left hand, he drew back his right hand and hit her hard across the face.

It was as well he had taken hold of her, for her head snapped back under the blow and her hands let go of the parapet. She cried out, and for a split second they swayed and Alec adjusted his balance to her weight. And then he felt her relax, her knees sagged, and she took hold again of the stone wall with normal, though trembling hands.

"I'm sorry, I had to do it," Alec explained. "You were hysterical."

She looked at him with brimming eyes, and nodded, and raised one trembling hand to her face. There was a scarlet mark right across it, and a trickle of blood where his signet ring had cut her above the cheek-bone. A tear or two overflowed her eyes from the hurt, but she was in her right mind again and accepted his explanation.

"Come on, let's get down. There must be an easier way." He looked around, assessing the possibilities against Sarah's state. Impossible to get her back down the way they had come up, he thought. The tower overhung slightly, and to get past the first bit would take a lot of nerve as well as physical strength. No, it would have to be the other way, down the inside of the tower – its overhang would be to their advantage then. "Come on, this way," he said, and was relieved to see that she was disposed to obey him.

He got over the side of the wall onto the inner ledge, and talking all the time guided Sarah onto the first foothold. She moved slowly and automatically as he spoke, doing exactly what he told her without a word, and he talked her down each step, looking out for both of them, keyed up to the task of picking a way that would not give under their weight. Luckily it was not too dark inside the tower, enough of the bright sunlight coming in through the original windows and other, unofficial, holes.

When they were about half way down he saw that she had recovered somewhat and was looking for her own foot- and hand-holds, and by the time they reached the bottom she was climbing normally and without his help. At last they stood on the rubble under which was blessed terra firma. Alec found his legs trembling from the effort, and his mind shaking with relief, and when Sarah turned towards him he grabbed her without thinking and pulled her against him.

"Thank God," he said. "Thank God I got you down." He held her tightly, pressing her head against him, and his eyes were closed against the images of what might have happened. After a moment he loosened his grasp a little to say,

"Let me see your poor face." He lifted her chin with one hand and smoothed the hair away from her cheek. The mark across it was still livid, and there was the beginnings of a raised bruise round the small cut. He gave a shaky laugh. "I very nearly gave you a black eye. Your poor little face. I must have hurt you. Yes, there are tear-stains." He touched the marks under her eyes, and stroked her cheeks and head, while her eyes looked into his wordlessly. With another laugh, nervous this time, he kissed her forehead, and then reluctantly let her go. "Come on," he said, taking her hand to help her down the heap of stones on which they were standing, "we'd better go and find Greig. He'll be beside himself."

He saw from her face that she had until that moment completely forgotten Greig, and it made even harder the effort he had just used not to kiss her as he held her in his arms. But the thought of Greig seemed finally to bring her back to herself, for as they stepped out into the sunshine she shook her hand free of his and said in a normal tone of voice,

"It was so strange, what happened up in the tower. I was quite all right, and then my body just went rigid, and I couldn't move. I wasn't frightened at all, not in my mind. I knew I was all right and I could get down quite easily, but I simply couldn't move."

"Yes," Alec said, "it's a form of hysteria I believe."

Greig was standing where Alec had left him, looking somehow shrunken with the fear that had possessed him this last quarter of an hour. When they came up to him he made a movement as if to take Sarah in his arms as Alec had, but stopped himself, and instead touched her cheek very gently with one finger.

"You'll have a bruise by tomorrow," he said. "What on earth were you doing up there?"

"I was looking at the view," Sarah said. "I was perfectly all right, I wasn't scared at all, it's just that I sort of froze up and couldn't move."

"You scared the life out of both of us," Greig said, beginning to be angry. "Why do you do these crazy things? You could have been killed – and killed someone else trying to rescue you."

"Or I might have fallen off the tower and squashed you – you were right underneath me," Sarah said sarcastically.

"It's no laughing matter," Greig shouted at her.

"It's no shouting matter either," Sarah shouted back. "I don't know why you're so indignant – you didn't get hurt."

"That's not the point. It's thoughtless and irresponsible of you to behave like that. I've every right to be angry."

"Don't you shout at me! You've no right at all to be angry. It wasn't you up on the tower. I was all right, I tell you. I'm perfectly capable of climbing up or down anything. It wasn't even you – "

Carried away by her anger, she only just realised in time what she was about, unforgiveably, to say. It wasn't even you that came up to fetch me. She knew how he was about heights, and she saw that he knew what she had been about to say. The anger in his eyes was replaced by hurt and some deeper and more complicated mixture of shame and sorrow. "I'm sorry," she said meekly. "I didn't mean to put anyone to any trouble."

"You should thank Alec for risking his life to save you," Greig said, and the slight emphasis on 'Alec' both drew attention to the fact that he was standing by listening to them quarrelling, and the fact that he knew the unfair comparison she had made in her mind moments before. He would not forgive her that easily.

"It's all right," Alec said awkwardly. "I wasn't really in

136

any danger. The tower's stronger than it looks. She'd just panicked, that's all."

Sarah's eyes were still fixed on Greig. "I'm sorry," she said again. "I shouldn't have gone up there. I'm sorry." Her voice was almost tearful at the second repetition. Greig's implacable stare took in her pleading eyes and her damaged, tearstained beauty, and he gave a curious little sigh, and drew her to him and kissed her.

"It's all right," he said, but his hands on her shoulders were impersonal, and the kiss was a strange, sad, almost fatherly kiss. He let her go, and the three of them stood facing each other, a little apart, not knowing what to do or say.

At that moment the little boy came scrambling over the ruins from the other side calling and beckoning to them, and pointing down the hill.

"I think it's time to go," Alec said. They walked after him to where Andreas stood holding the reins of his donkey. He confirmed Alec's words with,

"Time go back – you all ready?"

It seemed strange to them all that Andreas and his boy knew nothing of the drama that had been played out on the other side of the ruined monastery: but there had been no noise, no shouts or terrible crashes. He looked concerned at Sarah's cut face, and asked anxiously, "Missy hurt?"

"I fell," Sarah explained casually, and the other two kept silent. "It's nothing."

"No hurt?" Andreas enquired anxiously, and he felt his own arms and legs and then ribs as an example.

"No hurt," Sarah confirmed, and smiled to show him she was really all right.

"Fine, fine. We go back now. Missy – " and he gestured to a convenient stone from which she could mount her tiny steed. "You take fine pictures?" he asked confidently of the group at large.

'We haven't got a camera," Alec said, and then repeated it in Greek. Andreas' face was overspread with a kind of horror.

"No pictures?" he asked as if he could scarcely believe his ears. "You got no pictures?" He rolled up his eyes in horror and appealed to the saints to witness. Sarah was amused that he should think this such a grave omission. It must be the influence of American tourists, she thought. Having expressed his shock and regret to his own satisfaction, he called his boy and fired an order at him in rapid Greek, and the child looked at the English party, nodded, and raced off down the hill, followed by two of the dogs, barking madly.

"What was all that about?" Sarah asked Alec. "Where's he gone?"

"I don't know. He said something about photographs, but I can't understand when he talks as fast at that."

"Ask him," suggested Greig sensibly. "Andreas, where's your son gone?"

"Okay," Andreas nodded. "I get you fine picture. We go now."

The two statements seemed to conflict, but there seemed no purpose in asking more, so they mounted their donkeys, and the little procession moved off again in the same order, with the remaining two dogs trotting behind, their sole concession to the long journey.

When they reached the village again, the reason for the

138

boy's departure became clear, for they were met by him, together with a number of small children and dogs, and a young burly man holding a polaroid camera. Andreas greeted him and they exchanged information in rapid Greek. Then the young man came up to them and said in English,

"I am Mikhos, Andreas' son. I have a shop down in the village. My father tells me you have no camera, so cannot make a picture of this day to take home with you to England. So my father asks me to come and take a picture for you." He lifted his camera and showed them. "The picture comes at once and you can take away with you."

How thoughtful, Sarah thought, and how kind. They grouped themselves and Mikhos took the picture, and then they stood around waiting for it to be ready while Andreas and his small boys led the donkeys away.

"Now it is ready," said Mikhos, having timed it on his watch, and he pulled it out of his camera, peeled off the backing, and handed it to Sarah. Greig wanted to pay him for it, but he refused money, wished them well, and went away again to his shop. Andreas came back and Greig paid him for the afternoon, and gave him a tip as well, hoping that some of it might find its way to the kind son. They parted company with great friendliness, and the three visitors walked back towards the harbour and the path over the hill.

"Let me see the picture again," Alec said. Sarah handed it to him and looked at it again herself over his shoulder. It was all a part of the dream, and afterwards she could never look at it without feeling that way. She was in the centre, sitting on the little grey donkey, with her long hair shaken over one side of her face to hide her bruise. Greig stood on one side of the donkey, holding the reins, and looking into the camera with his usual gravity, while Alec stood on the other side, leaning one elbow familiarly on the donkey's wither, and grinning in *his* usual way.

Alec handed it to Greig, who looked at it, unsmiling. He didn't seem to draw any pleasant memories from it, and when he offered it back to Alec, saying, "Here, you'd better have it," Sarah thought perhaps it was the old enemy, jealousy, raising its head, because Alec looked so familiar and so much at ease in the picture. But Alec shook his head and refused it.

"I don't need it to remember today," he said. He gave Sarah a sideways look which she thought was meant to refer to the other photograph, but Greig intercepted the look and gave it his own interpretation, and looked graver still.

"Well, I certainly don't want it," he said. Sarah snatched it from him impatiently.

"I'll have it," she said. "After all the trouble the old man went to for us – the pair of you are ungrateful." And she put it away in her bag. But she felt that Greig was still hurt, from various things that had happened, and she did her best as they walked back over the hill to the villa to cheer him up, by talking to him, and keeping her arm linked firmly in his. She wanted him to know that though it was Alec who had climbed up the tower to rescue her, she did not feel that he, Greig, had let her down. And after all, it was Greig she was engaged to. But Greig was more silent even than was his usual nature, and in order to keep the talk going, Alec had to join in, or she would have been left to do all the talking. So, though she walked arm in arm with Greig, the conversation was all between her and Alec, which didn't really help matters at all.

When they reached the villa, they were all tired out, from various reasons, and though Alec tentatively suggested a drink they were all equally happy to go to their rooms.

"I think I'll have a bath and a rest before dinner," Sarah said.

"Good idea," Greig concurred. "I think I'll do the same. I'm covered in dust from that donkey-ride."

"You make it sound like Margate sands," Alec said, unable even in his state of thirst and tiredness to refrain from joking. "Well, I agree with you up to a point, but I'm so parched I have to have a drink before I get cleaned up. So if I can't prevail on either of you – " they shook their heads, in accord for once. "See you later, then, at dinner."

Alec went one way, and Greig and Sarah the other, towards their rooms. "I feel as if I could sleep for a week," Sarah said.

"You'll wake up once you've had a bath," Greig said. "It's probably delayed shock. Let me see your face again – turn to the light." Reluctantly she let him examine her cheek. "He must have fetched you a hell of a crack," he concluded. Sarah had not wanted to bring up the subject of Alec's hitting her, for fear of Greig's reaction, but he seemed quite calm, and she was glad to have got it over with.

"Did you see?" she asked.

"No. I guessed. I suppose it was necessary – "

"I think so. I couldn't move until he did."

" – but he didn't have to hit you so hard. What made the cut?"

"His ring, he said."

"It's lucky it wasn't nearer your eye. You look enough like a prize-fighter. He didn't have to hit you that hard. A nice enough chap, but a little over-enthusiastic."

Damning, with faint praise, thought Sarah. We'd better cross Alec off our list of conversational topics. He's too dangerous. "I hope there's something decent for dinner," she said. "I'm starving." It was a random choice, but not fortunate.

"I hope so too. I hope there isn't another barbecue," Greig said. They walked the rest of the way to their rooms in silence and parted at the door to Sarah's. She made one last try.

"If you're not ashamed to be seen walking in with a prize-fighter, will you call for me on the way to dinner?"

Greig's expression softened, and he patted her sound cheek. "Of course I will," he said. "Some prize-fighters are quite pretty, after all. So they tell us."

For Greig it was not bad, and definitely an effort. They parted friends, and Sarah hoped that Alec would not take it into his head to torment them further that night.

CHAPTER ELEVEN

Alec was already seated at his table in the dining room when Sarah and Greig came in, and Sarah hoped he would stay there; but after exchanging a friendly nod from a distance, he came over to their table and asked politely and kindly after Sarah's welfare. She replied as politely, but with considerably less enthusiasm, and to her relief he took the hint and went back to his own table. He gave her, however, a look of peculiar intensity, and a smile that Greig could hardly help noticing.

After a few moments silence, during which the waiter placed a bowl of salad and a bottle of retsina before them, Greig said,

"How well do you know that chap?"

Sarah's heart turned over, but she kept her countenance, and after toying briefly with the idea of a flippant reply, said seriously,

"Not at all." Neither she nor Greig wanted to meet the other's eye, and it was convenient to concentrate their attention on the food and wine. "After all," she went on, "I've only met him one time that you haven't, and that was on the boat that day."

"What did you talk about?"

"I don't remember," she said with rising annoyance. "Probably the scenery. Why all the questions?"

Greig looked up at that point, and had Sarah not been expecting him to be jealous, she might have noticed a different expression on his face.

"Why so worried about all the questions?" he asked.

"I'm not *worried*," she said hastily. "I just wonder what there is so fascinating about him that you keep on talking about him, that's all." They say the best method of defence is attack, but it also gives away the fact that you feel there is something to defend.

"I'll tell you," Greig said with energy. "It's just that once or twice I've seen you and him exchanging a funny sort of look, as if you've got some secret between you – " he got no further. Sarah, from the stimulus of guilt, flared up.

"Don't be ridiculous – how can we have a secret! I've only met him once more than you, and that was in an open public place with a couple of dozen other people looking on. What on earth do you think we could get up to in a situation like that?"

"Don't fly off the handle – " Greig said, lifting a hand in a gesture of peace.

"I've every right to fly off the handle! Your stupid jealousy will be the ruin of everything if you keep on giving in to it like this."

"Forget it," Greig said flatly. His nostrils were white with restrained emotion, and it was obvious that they could not go any further than this without a public scene.

"Yes, it's all very well to say forget it when you've – "

"I said forget it," Greig said again, this time with a quiet

144

force she could not ignore. "Drop the subject." There was a silence, and then he went on, with an obvious effort at reconciliation, "Let's not quarrel. We're both on edge after today – let's relax and enjoy the evening."

Softened, Sarah gave him an uncertain smile, to which he responded, and then lifted his glass to her.

"Cheers!"

"Cheers," she said, and felt her hackles lowering, and her blood cooling.

Though the atmosphere had been less than festive at their table, the same was not true of the dining room in general, and when they were able to emerge from their own affairs, they found the usual kind of party feeling building up. This was partly due to the habit of the waiters of bringing more wine to the tables when there was a wait for the next course, which meant that the diners drank themselves into a good humour, and hardly noticed the excellence of the moussaka and the garlic bread when it did arrive. Three waiters happening to arrive at the same part of the dining room at the same moment, they linked their arms together and began to sing a close-harmony folk song with which went a little four-step dance. The guests stopped talking to watch. One or two knew the chorus well enough to join in; others clapped the rhythm, which became faster and faster until the three dancers could hardly sing for panting.

The dance and song ended together on a loud shout, and there was a burst of laughing and clapping. The service grew more erratic after that as first one waiter and then another was prevailed upon for another song. They managed to get round by occasionally asking one of the guests to sing instead, but the hour grew later and the dining room did not clear, and most of the guests were well enough lubricated to need little encouragement to get up on their chairs or even the tables and dance. Someone dashed out and fetched their guitar; one of the staff brought out an accordion; bottles of wine continued somehow to arrive at the tables. The french windows onto the verandah were open, and the cheerful noise drifted out onto the scented night, surprising the tree frogs into silence.

Some of the guests formed a line and began a Greek version of the conga, and as it passed their table, Sarah was drawn into it, leaving Greig laughing at his own escape and tapping out the rhythm with a fork-handle on the table. The line wound round the dining room, collecting more people as it went, and then like an unwieldy snake writhed out onto the verandah and worked its way round the villa and into the olive grove, with the accordionist and other onlookers running alongside to keep up. Sarah was not entirely surprised when Alec inched into the line behind her and breathed hello into her ear.

"Oh, it's you," she said.

"That's not much of a greeting," he protested. "Having a good time? We ought to get someone to take photographs to remind us of this wonderful moment."

"Don't talk to me about photographs!" Sarah shouted at him above the noise. "I've already had one quarrel with Greig about you tonight."

"Have you really? I'm flattered. I wonder what he'd say if I showed him this?" And he freed one hand from her waist to dip into his breast pocket for the snap that was the beginning of it all.

"Don't you dare!" she said. She ought to have believed he was only joking, but there was a streak of devilment in him.

"Why not? It's a nice picture. I think he'd be very interested."

"Give it to me!" Sarah cried, making a vain snatch at it. Alec lifted it just beyond her reach.

"Certainly not. I paid good money for this. Anyway, I want to keep it to remind me of a pleasant day. I'll let anyone have a look that wants, though – Greig or anyone."

"Give it to me!"

"No – not on any account." But he let it almost into her grasp before jerking it away again, to encourage her. She made another snatch, and he broke out of the line, laughing, and waving the photograph derisively. Sarah went after him, and he ran, dodging in and out of the trees, leading her on and away from the other guests until he had coaxed her out onto the cliff top above the quiet sea. There he turned as if at bay, and as she ran at him he held his hand up high so that she had to jump to try to reach it. With the excitement of the chase, the wine, and the party feeling that had gone before, Sarah had almost forgotten the purpose of the pursuit and was laughing as she used one hand on Alec's shoulder to try to push herself up high enough to reach the photograph.

And then Alec's arm was round her like a vice, pressing her against him, and she caught one startled glimpse of his face above her before his mouth came down on hers, crushing her lips with a passion that held no laughter. A tremor that was almost fear ran down her spine and she struggled to pull away, but his other arm went round her to hold her close to him, so that she felt the heat of his body through her thin dress. Her blood raced madly about her body, and her thoughts grew confused. She only knew that she could not resist as whole-heartedly as she ought, that her hands on his shoulders were pulling him closer, not pushing him away.

At last he stopped, perhaps to draw breath, and allowed her head to fall back a little. Behind him a great silver moon sailed clear in the dark starry sky, throwing a metallic path across the still sea, and leaving his face in shadow. Sarah could only see the glint of his eyes and the outline of his head, but she knew his face without seeing it. And when he spoke, she knew the exact expression of suppressed humour that would quirk his lips at the corners.

"That'll teach you to look at me like that," he said, then – "I'll give you the photograph – for another kiss like that."

It brought her back to reality with a bump. She jerked away from him sharply enough to free herself, and stood facing him with her pulses racing.

"That was a dirty trick," she said. "How dare you blackmail me?"

"Oh, is that what you call it? I call it fair exchange – barter, if you like."

"I call it blackmail. You can keep the picture."

"And show it to your worthy boyfriend?"

He was joking, but Sarah was too angry to realise. "That proves what I say. A trick worthy of you. Fair exchange indeed. No, if it's fair exchange you want, I'll *buy* it from you. For twice what you paid."

"No money could buy this photograph," he said, and now he was angry too, his joke having been turned into something more serious than either of them could have wanted. "I've told you my price – it's up to you. In any case, he must be wondering by now where you are – "

That realisation crossed Sarah's mind at the same moment, and without another word to Alec she turned on her heel and ran back towards the villa. She had no idea how long she had been away, or what had become of the rest of the dance line, but she was relieved to find when she returned that the party was still going strong, with people coming and going and dancing both in the dining room and out on the verandah, so she hoped to slip in unobtrusively. Greig was still at their table, with a glass of wine in his hand and tapping his fingers on the table to the music. He smiled as she appeared, and said,

"I've been wondering where you were. I hoped you'd come back for me."

Sarah gave him a shaky smile in return and said,

"I was having a look at the sea. How about a swim? There's a lovely moon, and it's very warm."

Greig smiled willingly. "That's a good idea," he said. "We'll go and get our things, shall we?" He stood up, and looked at her with faint concern. "Are you okay? You look a bit odd."

Sarah composed her face. "Too much wine, I expect. A swim will sober me up."

They fetched their bathing costumes and towels and walked together but without touching down the cliff steps to the small white beach, deserted now, and glimmering white in the moonlight. The sand was still warm from the heat of the day, and the air was still. They changed with their backs to each other, and when they turned round again, Greig had his first view of Sarah's new costume. Though evidently moved, he said only,

"It's a good job there's no-one else on the beach."

"Don't you like it?" she asked with small disappointment.

"Like it?" he hesitated. "It's stunning. Too much for me." She didn't quite know what he meant, but thought it safer to take it as approval, and with relief for his kindness she slipped her hand into his and they walked together down to the sea's lip. It was as warm as new milk, scarcely turning over, with a gentle sound like a sigh, and as they waded forwards, Sarah gave a cry of surprise. Where the water folded back against her thighs, it was shining green-gold like liquid fire.

"What is it?" she said, turning her hand through and back to catch a spark of it.

"Phosphorescence," Greig said; Sarah smiled up at him – he always had the answers for her. "It think it's something to do with the heat – at any rate, you only get it in the summer, and in places like this. Strange, isn't it?"

"And beautiful," she said. Her other hand remained in Greig's until they reached water deep enough to swim, and then they lay forward languidly onto the water that was like a cushion of silk and swam out towards the mouth of the bay.

Above them the sky was pinpricked with stars. "I've never seen so many," Sarah said. "You just wouldn't believe there could be so many."

"You don't see them in the town, because of the street lamps," Greig told her. The Milky Way was spun across the dome of the night like mist, or a drift of spun sugar, and the moon sailed high, carrying with it its own patch of electric-blue clear sky. They rolled over onto their backs and floated, moving only enough to maintain their position.

"It's so lovely here," Sarah said. "I wish I could stay for ever."

"Do you?" Greig said.

"Don't you?"

"No. It *is* lovely, but I don't confuse it with reality. It *is* only a holiday, after all, and whatever happens here, real life is much more exciting and much more worth taking trouble with."

"Real life. You mean, back home, work, your career and so on."

"That's real life," Greig consented. "There's only just so much room for moonlight and so on."

Sarah sighed. "I don't see it that way. I'd like the whole of life to be like this – just drifting from one enchanted place to another."

Greig didn't answer, and she knew that he didn't want to spoil her moment for her. He was her dear friend, who cared for her and knew her, despite all their quarrels.

"Oh, the moon's going in," she said with disappointment a moment later.

"Not for long," Greig assured her. "Only a passing patch of cloud. Look, you can see the edges of it."

"Oh yes – all silver. That must be the cloud with the silver lining."

"*Every* cloud has a silver lining, silly."

"So it has; I'd forgotten."

"And in the metaphorical sense, the silver lining to this one is that you can see the phosphorescence much better when it's darker."

"So you can," Sarah said, turning herself upright with some splashing. Every movement sent ripples of it flowing outwards from them. They plunged their hands into the water and drew it up between their fingers, long trailers of green fire; Sarah scooped up handfuls and poured it over Greig, watching it run down him in cold dripping flames into the glittering sea. They splashed each other and laughed, their voices hardly echoing on the still air.

And then suddenly they were no longer alone in the water. They had drifted rather a long way out, and were treading water beyond the bay-mouth, when a score of black humps rose silently round them, and the nearest to Sarah made a sharp sighing sound, startling her.

"What are they – dolphins?" she asked Greig, stretching out her hand to the shining black curve. Phoo! It cleared its blow hole and evaded her touch effortlessly.

"Porpoises," Greig said. "Dolphins have snouts. It's a whole school." Turning on the spot and smiling with delight, Sarah watched as they surged around her, dipping and rising, and sometimes leaping clean out of the sea in a perfect curve that dripped green-gold light. They were all around them, playing with the small waves, surging and sighing as if with the most exquisite pleasure. Sarah and Greig swam with them, sometimes almost touching them, but never quite. The sea crumpled against their black bows like the softest tissue, their backs glittered with phosphorescence; it was as if a performance had been put on specially for Sarah and Greig.

The moon appeared again, riding clear of the clouds, and as if that were their cue the porpoises turned away from the shore and raced away with their graceful bobbing movement, out to sea again.

"Like rocking-sea-horses," Sarah said, watching them disappear with regret.

"We're rather a long way out," Greig said. "We'd better swim back in."

"I'm tired," Sarah said. "I could sleep right now, right here. It's like a warm, soft bed. I'm sure it would support me."

"Don't try it," Greig warned her. They swam back slowly. Sarah's breast-stroke grew more languid as the wine and fatigue of the day combined to make her sleepy, and she felt she was making no progress against the weight of the water. Greig had to help her, swimming slowly beside her to break the water for her, encouraging her. The shore sloped gently there, and long before she was within her depth he could put his feet down, and then he towed her in until she, too, could stand.

"Dear Greig," she said as she stumbled through the shallows to the sand. "Always there to help me."

153

"Not quite always," he said quietly, but she didn't hear him. He had not been able to help her at the ruins.

She stood like a child as he dried her with her towel. "Don't bother to get dressed here. It'll be quicker to go up like this and get straight into your nightdress in your room. I can't do much with your hair, I'm afraid – there's too much of it. I'll just wrap your towel round it so it doesn't drip on you."

"It needs washing anyway. I'll do it tomorrow," she said, and took the towel from his hands when his unskilled attempts failed to make it stay in place round her head. They walked up the steps, Greig holding her hand and helping her on. "Delayed shock," he said. "You'll be fine after a good sleep." They went in at the side door to avoid the party that was still going on at the front of the villa, and finally stopped at the door to Sarah's room.

"Goodnight then – have a good sleep," Greig said, Sarah turned to him and put up her arms to be hugged, and he did, but gently, almost distantly.

"Dear Greig," she said, half asleep now. "You're my dear friend. You'll always be there, won't you?"

"Always," he said, kissing her forehead. "Dry your hair a bit before you fall into bed, won't you. Goodnight Sarah." And he put her away from him gently but firmly. "Go on to bed now."

"'Night," she said, and went in to her room. Greig closed the door after her, and for some moments stood where he was, looking at the closed door with a thoughtful, almost sad expression. Then he sighed heavily and went to his own room. He looked at his own bed, and

154

shook his head, as if he knew sleep was not for him. For a moment longer he pondered, and then he sat down and drew his study books firmly towards him and, chin in hand, began to read.

CHAPTER TWELVE

The next morning Sarah woke early, feeling absolutely refreshed and full of vigour, and she went straight away and banged on Greig's door cheerfully to see if he'd like to swim before breakfast. On their way through the house Sarah spotted a notice on the board with details of a trip that day to a neighbouring island, and she stopped and read it with interest.

"An uninhabited island," she read. "Al-fresco lunch – bathing and fishing – return for dinner here. Sounds fun. It's an all-day trip, though, what a pity."

"Why a pity?" Greig asked. Sarah looked at him with an expression that said, don't ask the obvious, and he smiled sheepishly. "I sat up last night after you'd gone to bed and did quite a bit of work, so I think I could take another day off. Mind you – " and he tried to look stern and failed, "don't expect it every day. I don't want to spoil you."

"You sat up last night?" she exclaimed with astonishment. "You're crazy! It must have been midnight by the time we came up from the beach. What time did you go to bed?"

"Oh, I don't remember," he said off-handedly. "I

suppose about three or four. I don't really know."

"Three or four! But it's only half-past six now!" She clapped her hand to her mouth with the realisation. "And I went and woke you up, banging on the door! You must be exhausted! Go back to bed, you fool, and get an hour or two in."

"Don't be silly. It would only make me feel worse, to sleep for an hour and then have to get up. I'm up now, and a swim will refresh me. I can last through until tonight now."

Sarah argued, but he would not be persuaded. "Well," she said at last, "you're very noble, and I shall feel suitably guilty all day. If I hadn't come and thumped you up, you might have slept until lunchtime."

"Then you wouldn't have been able to go on your trip, and *I'd* have felt guilty at keeping you hanging round the villa all morning doing nothing."

"That would have been no hardship. I can always sit and read a book on the beach until it gets too hot. Still, if you're sure – I'd much rather go to this island."

After all the alarms and bickerings of the day before, they seemed to be perfect friends today, and she wanted to keep it that way, which was why she was particularly anxious not to have any brushes with Alec Russell. It was too much, however, to hope that he would not be on the trip, and she was neither pleased nor surprised when she and Greig boarded the *Penelope* down at the harbour to see him already on board and possessed of a good place in the bows. He waved a greeting to them both. Greig said hello with his usual grave politeness, but Sarah gave him a cold look, to which he responded behind Greig's back with a malicious grin and a significant tap at his breast pocket. Sarah coloured at the obvious meaning and turned away.

Jorkos came aboard with his general accompaniment of shouts and jokes, and soon they had cast off and were heading out to sea, a sea that lifted under the bows gently like curves of mobile blue glass. The water was so clear that as they hung over the side of the boat they could see down to the bottom, to the pale sand and the strange vegetable growth, and the occasional cloud of rainbow-coloured fish. It was a long trip, and across open sea, with little to see except the occasional seabird or diver. Sarah could never be bored when she was near the sea, and with looking at the water, and enjoying the vivid blue of the sky and the warmth of the sun, and wondering anew how Jorkos could steer his boat with no landmarks and, apparently, no compass, and talking to him about the island they were to visit, she had plenty to occupy her.

Greig was less easily pleased, and once they were into deep water where the weed grew, and he could no longer see the bottom, he lost interest and took out a book. It would have made Sarah sigh with impatience at another time, but she was determined today that they should be at peace with each other and left him with a smile to enjoy himself his way while she enjoyed herself in hers.

"What's the attraction about this island?" she asked Jorkos as she perched on a box beside his wheelhouse and examined with pleasure her deepening tan. She was simply dressed today in blue jeans and a white teeshirt, and an apricot scarf to tie her salty hair back, but it showed up the butter brown of her arms and face.

"It's a very small island, nothing much. Mr. Geralds boughts it two years ago, so we use it a lot. It's gots a beach, fine for swimming, and a streams with fish, fine for fishing, and lots of birds, lots of flowers. It's a nice place."

Alec, whose persistent gaze she had been avoiding since they came on board, strolled as if casually over to where she was sitting and under cover of asking Jorkos how long it would take them to get there, cornered Sarah.

"I get the impression you're avoiding me," he said.

"What ever gave you that impression?" she said sarcastically, "I'd be grateful if you'd leave me alone today. I'd like to have a quiet day with my fiancé without quarrelling again."

Alec shot a look at Greig, absorbed in his book despite the glories of the sea and sky around him.

"It looks like being quiet," he said. "It strikes me you'll be glad of a little company later."

"Never mind that," Sarah said urgently. "If he looks up and sees you talking to me it'll start it all off again."

"But you forget, I want to start it off," Alec said, his eyes glinting. "I'd like to get into conversation with him, so that I can bring it round to the subject of photography. I see he's got a camera with him today. That would be a good way to start a conversation, wouldn't it?" and with that he left her and went across to where Greig was sitting. Sarah saw them exchange a few words, and when she saw Alec's hand go to his breast pocket she could restrain herself no longer and jumped up to rush and intervene.

But she had not moved a pace before she saw that what he had taken out of his pocket was a tube of sweets, which he offered to Greig, and then took one himself. The fact that he glanced back at Sarah showed he knew what effect he was likely to have on her. She turned her head away indignantly, refusing to return his grin of delight in what he found an amusing situation.

"He bothering you?" Jorkos asked softly, startling her. She looked up and saw his small shiny eyes bright with sympathy. How much had he worked out for himself, from their exchanges and Sarah's red cheeks?

"It's all right," she said. "He thinks it's funny."

"If he bothers you, you tells me and I fix him."

"I'll tell you if he does," Sarah promised.

At last the island appeared, a heap of red-gold rocks crumpled in the sea like rose-petals, and topped with stunted olives. They rounded the rocks and came to the bay, at the point of which was a crude jetty built of wood to which Jorkos intended tying up the boat. The bay was almost circular, the mouth being very narrow, with the usual white sand. Higher up from the beach was an olive grove, and between the trees and the beach were sand dunes that were covered with a green-and-cream froth of lilies which filled the air with a rich and heady scent.

Sarah, standing beside Greig who had put his book away again, was entranced. "Isn't it beautiful!" she cried, feeling that she was running out of expressions strong enough for the places she was seeing. "I would never have believed lilies would grow in sand like that."

"Grass does," Greig said reasonably. "And anyway, I should imagine there's water fairly close under the surface, judging by that stream." He pointed to the silver snake that wound from a low place beween the dunes at the other end of the bay and ran down to the sea across the beach, sending many little tributaries to carve their own narrow channels between banks of red reeds.

"That must be where the fishing is," Sarah said. "And that raft in the middle of the bay I suppose is for swimmers."

"Don't you know?" Greig asked, amused. "I would have thought you'd have had every detail out of Jorkos by now."

"Not quite," she smiled. "But he did say this island belongs to the villa, so I expect there will be lots of little arrangements like that set up here. I should think they built this jetty, for instance."

The *Penelope* was tied up, rocking on the gentle swell, and the guests went ashore, full of eager exclamations at the unexpected scene before them, the beautiful back-drop of the lillies, intensely green and white against the intensely blue sky. Up in the olive grove, discreetly hidden so that they didn't spoil the scene, were a number of wooden and stone huts, built by the original owners and added to by the new, where various amenities were provided. Members of the villa staff who had come along to help pointed out the two changing huts and the toilets, and unlocked the store in which was kept the equipment such as fins and snorkels, and traditional tridents for spearing fish in the stream.

The guests soon scattered to enjoy themselves in their own particular ways. Some went straight into the water to bathe, swimming out to the raft to practise diving,

161

or splashing or basking in the shallows. The confirmed sun-worshippers spread themselves out on the white sand to bake a little, armed with suntan oil, dark glasses, and insect repellent. Those who had come to fish armed themselves with tridents and waded up the stream where the fish butted against their legs as if asking to be caught.

Jorkos had his own duties to attend to, and with the assistance of a couple of boys he set about preparing the fire in the small brick-built furnace on the beach. They carried the big bulbous flasks of wine down to the water's edge and wedged them between the rocks to keep cool. Soon a wisp of smoke rose from the furnace, and the smell of woodsmoke drifted across the beach, a pungent counterpoint to the sleepy smell of the lilies. Jorkos stripped to the waist, the sweat running down under his matted black hair so that he looked like a wet bear as he attended to the cooking. The boys meanwhile prepared baskets of vegetables and ran back and forth for more wood.

Sarah and Greig, in common with other guests who were neither bent on fishing, toasting or swimming, walked about admiring and exploring. In the olive grove behind the dunes it was cooler, and after they had stood watching a pair of goldfinches for a while, Greig said he felt like staying there, in the shade, reading.

"I might go in for a swim in a bit, but I'd just like to relax for a while," he said apologetically. "Why don't you get changed and go in, and I'll join you later?"

Sarah shook her head. "I'll wait until you go in. I don't want to swim on my own. I expect we'll be eating soon, anyway. I'll just explore until then."

162

She walked out through the grove to the other side, and found there a small lake where the stream spread out on its way down to the sea. It was surrounded all round by thick reed beds, and she stepped back quickly when she discovered her feet sinking into marshy ground. Obviously one could not get right down to the edge here; she backed off until she found a place dry and firm enough to sit, and there she remained, quietly watching the extraordinary variety of wild creatures that lived in and around the lake. She kept so still that after a while the creatures would pass quite close to her, and she had a fascinating time counting all the different inhabitants of the area. There were all kinds of water fowl, and partridges and snipe and quail, water rats to make her think of home and terrapins, like halved chocolate easter-eggs, and brown water-snakes, to make her realise she was far away.

She was watching, with amusement, a pair of wood-pigeons crashing about after each other with the clumsiness of their kind when Alec found her.

"Here you are," he said with satisfaction, she looked up in surprise which quickly turned to annoyance.

"Must you follow me everywhere?" she asked. "I thought I might be left in peace here."

"If you want to hide in the reeds you'll have to wear something that blends in more. That white top and yellow scarf make you stand out a mile away."

"It isn't yellow, it's apricot. What do you want?"

"I thought you might like some company."

"I don't. Goodbye."

"He's left you alone again, then? Where is he this time?"

"He's reading. And I wish you'd *go away*."

"Do you?" Alec asked, suddenly serious. "Do you really?" She looked up at him then, at his brown face and fox-coloured hair, his laughing eyes, and his long, mobile mouth – the mouth that had kissed her so fiercely only the night before. She felt the blood drain from her face. Why did he torment her so? "Yes, go away," she said, and her voice was almost tearful. He opened his mouth to reply, but what he would have said was lost for ever as a loud clanging noise came from the region of the beach, sending a cloud of pigeons up with a clatter of wings from the olive grove.

"What on earth is that?" she asked, startled.

"I imagine it's an improvised gong – I should say lunch is ready. Are you coming?"

"When I'm ready. Please go and leave me alone."

For a wonder he did as he was asked. "Don't leave it too late, or everything will be eaten," he said, and trotted away between the trees.

Sarah followed slowly, far enough behind him not to catch up, and collected Greig from the place she had left him.

"Was that the dinner gong?" he asked as she appeared beside him. "Good, I'm hungry."

He seemed not to notice that she was silent as they walked down to the beach and joined the crowd round the cooking fire. Jorkos was soaked now to the waist, but grinning happily, refreshing himself with draughts from a flask of wine beside him. The young people squatted or sat or reclined at their ease and the food was piled on a tarpaulin and handed round with cheerful words and

164

smiles. The wine, cool from the water, was fetched, and tasted no worse for being drunk from paper cups. The fish came fresh from the griddle, the skin charred black and beginning to flake off, showing the delicate white flesh underneath; it was passed round, and seasoned with a drop of lemon juice or a sprinkle of black pepper and eaten with flinching fingers.

There were baskets of bread, and of fruit and vegetables in circulation from which everyone helped himself, and the conversation grew lively as the first edge of appetite was dulled. Those who had been fishing boasted of their skill or rued their failure, and commented favourably or otherwise on the quality of the fish they were eating. This led to stories of other fishing expeditions and jokes in plenty on the piscatorial art and its enthusiasts.

Greig and Sarah didn't talk. She thought he was probably tired, and didn't try to converse, but she found her eyes drawn again and again to the noisiest, happiest group, at the centre of which was Alec. Why she should have felt resentful that someone else was enjoying his company when she had sent him away, she didn't ask herself. But hard as she tried to keep her attention on the food, it would wander towards that voice and that smile.

Now small joints of mixed fowl were coming from the fire, and Sarah found herself with a wing of what turned out to be pigeon, which she ate turn and turn about with fruit from the basket, delicious ripe figs and grapes. She wondered if some future party from the villa would eat with as much relish the pair of pigeons she had seen lovemaking that day, but the thought didn't sadden her; it seemed as good an end as any. Gradually the eating slowed down, and with it the talking, and everyone discovered how hot it was out in the sun and near the fire, and people began to drift away to the shade of the trees, or to the shallows to cool off. She moved with Greig to the edge of the olive grove, but no sooner had he stretched out on his back with his arms under his head than he fell asleep, so she was deprived again of his company.

For a moment she looked down at his sleeping face. He certainly needed and deserved this nap, having had no more than a couple of hours the night before, and he looked so peaceful that she could not resent being left alone again. It really was tremendously hot, and having rested long enough to let her meal settle, she stripped off her outer clothes and padded down to the water's edge in her bathing suit to cool off. The sun burned like a great white flower in the cornflower blue sky, and after a few moments lolling in the shallows she found even that did not answer, and slipping over onto her front she pushed off and swam slowly out to the raft, anchored in the middle of the bay.

On the far side of it there was a patch of shadow thrown by the raft itself, and by hanging to the ropes there she could keep her whole body under water without having the top of her head scorched by the sun. It was delicious, and she moved her legs idly in the water, relishing the coolness and watching with a now familiar amusement as the small fishes butted against her, mouthing at the salt of her skin.

She heard a swimmer approaching from the other side of the raft – the side nearest the shore – and knew

166

without even having to see that it was Alec again. He would probably come the same way round the raft as she had, so she thought that by continuing round in the same direction she could avoid him and swim back to the shore. While she was edging round hand over hand, however, the raft heaved and bucked as the swimmer climbed up on top. Seconds later he was looking down at her over the edge.

"Hello," he said. She gave him a resentful look and made to push off from the raft to swim away, but with the swift movement of a fish his brown hands darted out and closed over hers. "Don't go away. I've brought out two sets of snorkelling gear. I thought I'd show you the wonders of the deep, as I suggested the first day – do you remember?"

"Yes, I remember," she said. She looked at him quizzically, as if wondering what sort of mood he was in this time, and he smiled at her in his most charming way. "Your boyfriend is asleep, and you need some company, and I promise not to tease you," he said gently. "You'll love seeing under the water. Come on up." And he pulled at her hand encouragingly. He was right, she did want company; and especially, she wanted *his* company.

"Promise," she said doubtfully.

"Promise," he said, and bracing himself he pulled her up onto the raft. He helped her fit the flippers and adjust them to hold tightly. "You'll get terrible blisters if they are loose enough to rub," he warned. Then he showed her how to wet her mask so it wouldn't steam up, and instructed her on how to beathe through the snorkel.

167

"You'll be all right," he said. "Just remember whatever you do, not to breathe through your nose."

She nodded, and they slipped over the side together into the warm water, already a grateful relief from the heat of the sun in which they had been sitting for five minutes. For the first few minutes they swam round in circles while Sarah got used to the – to her – rather scary experience of breathing through the snorkel tube, and to keeping her body level in the water, and driving steadily with her flippers. Then they came up for a brief rest, and Alec said,

"We'll see the best things over there by the rocks. Are you all right now? Okay then, stay with me, and keep your eyes open."

Head down, slowly they ploughed across the silky bay, watching and watched by the shoals of small fish. Below them passed a continuous stream of water life and vegetation, weed like black trees, weed like emerald ribbons, weed as red as blood or bloated and anaemic with bulging blisters that needed popping. Between the weed beds were patches of white sand and clumps of rock where lived hermits and plate-crabs and sea slugs and brown fat snakes with golden bellies and starfish of more different colours and designs than Sarah could have dreamed of in a lifetime.

There were shells of all shapes and colours, some empty and some inhabited, and anemones, open and seductive to the pale, amorphous small things that swam innocently by. Slowly they made for the rocks, drawing each other's attention to various wonders with a tug at the arm and a jab of the finger, and when they reached their objective they came up for a breather, holding on to the rocks over which the water broke without force and wiping the water from their mouths.

"Isn't it wonderful!" Sarah exclaimed, panting. "I'd love to go down properly, with breathing tanks, I mean, so that I could go down and touch things. Have you ever?"

"Yes, I go scuba diving in England, though it's more fun where the water's warmer, of course. Still, the one thing you can say about English waters is that you're not likely to get eaten or stung to death."

"Are you here?" Sarah asked, alarmed, looking behind her as if she half expected a marauding shark.

"Not right here," he said, laughing. "Anyway, I'd soon tell you if there was anything bad around. Don't you trust me?"

"Not a lot," she said, but avoided his eyes. She didn't want to get off the subject of diving and onto a subject more dangerous. "Gosh, my mouth feels about a foot wide. This rubber thing's no fun – worse than going to the dentist."

"Want to stop?"

"In a bit. Let's have one more go first."

"All right. It's shallow here, so you'll be able to actually pick up things from the bottom that interest you – only I don't recommend any of the larger crabs."

"I shall treat them with the respect they deserve," she said, and they readjusted their masks and duck-dived under the water again. They didn't do much swimming now, but simply lay on the surface looking down, drawing themselves along by the rock and weed towards the shore, and examining anything that caught their fancy. Sarah had rather a yen for some of the shells, but every time she picked one up there turned out to be someone in it, and she wouldn't harm them. Alec, being more confident, sometimes dived down further to pick up something to show her, clearing his snorkel when he came up again with a sharp snort that reminded her of the porpoises. He managed to find one or two shells which she approved under water with a thumbs up, and then the water was getting to be too shallow and they came up again.

Alec could stand, but Sarah had to tread water as she dragged off her mask, with a half-laughing sigh of relief. She rubbed at her stretched mouth ruefully, and pushed back her long soaking hair so that it floated free behind her, as she clung with one hand to a bunch of tough seaweed that grew from the rock.

"Phew! Am I glad to breathe something that doesn't smell of rubber. It's a pity they can't make those things out of something that smells of roses or fresh bread or coffee or something." Alec didn't answer, and looking up she saw that he was looking at her with an expression that made her heart turn over. Nervously she stammered on. "Have you got those shells? Let me have a look at them – must have some kind of souvenir from the sea bed, mustn't I?"

Alec paid no attention to her jabbering, and when she held out her free hand for the shells he closed his own over it tightly.

"Alec, don't," she said in a subdued voice.

"You look like a mermaid," he said huskily, "and your hair like floating goldy-brown weed."

"I don't think I care to have my hair called seaweed,"

170

she said, trying for a joke, then, "do you have to keep hold of my hand?"

He looked down at it as if he didn't know what it was, and then tightened his grip, and reached a hand over her shoulder and wound it in her floating hair. "Yes, I do," he said, "I really think I do."

"Some one might see," Sarah said. Her heart was fluttering madly, but he was not to know that. She was hanging on harder to the weed, having quite forgotten to tread water. "Greig might wake up and stroll out this way – oh!" At that point her hand slipped off the clump of weed she was holding and she was plunged down into the water; and in a move as instinctive to both, she grabbed at Alec, flinging her arms round his neck, and he put his arms round her and lifted her up and towards him. Their wet bodies were pressed together, their faces almost touching, and it was quite instinctive for him to attempt to kiss her, but she jerked her head away furiously.

"Don't you dare,' she cried. "You'd take advantage of me? Let me go!" Alec hesitated a second, and then did as she asked – literally. She went under, swallowed some water, but recovered herself quickly, came up coughing, and took a fresh hard hold on the weed. "Don't you dare laugh, either," she warned him as soon as she could speak. He had been openly grinning at her plight, but now his face grew serious again.

"Sarah," he said, "why don't you be honest with your-self?"

"I always am," she said indignantly.

"I don't think so," he said. "You look at me with inviting eyes, but when I try to kiss you you push me

171

away. You tell me to go away, but if I don't you stay with me. What do you want of me?"

Offended pride sparked Sarah's anger. "*All* I want of you," she said stiffly, "is that photograph."

"And that's all?" She nodded. "And why do you want it? What will you do with it?"

"Tear it up, and burn the pieces," she said promptly. Alec thought for a moment.

"All right," he said. "I'll give it to you – on one condition."

"I don't want to hear your conditions," she said haughtily.

"I don't mean anything like that," he said with some dignity. "There's a dance at the villa when we get back tonight. I'll give it to you sometime during the dance – on the condition that you destroy it there and then, in front of me."

"Is that all?" she asked, surprised. She didn't understand what the catch was, and she couldn't believe there wasn't one.

"That's all."

"Then why can't you give it to me now? Why wait until tonight?"

"Because I haven't got it with me, Brain," he said.

"Oh," she said in a small voice. Then, "but how will I get away from Greig?"

"That's your business. It's nothing to do with me. Well, are you on?"

"Yes, all right. I don't see the point of all this, but I agree."

"Okay. Now if you'll yank off your flippers and give

172

them to me, I'll take this gear back. Here are your shells, by the way."

"Oh, thanks. They are beautiful, aren't they."

"Yes, they are beautiful," Alec said, but he wasn't looking at the shells.

CHAPTER THIRTEEN

Sarah was so glad to be near the end of the troublesome episode of the photograph that she was lighthearted all the rest of the day. When she left Alec at the water's edge and ran back up to the place where she had left Greig, she found him just waking, sticky-eyed and fuddle-headed from sleeping in the heat.

"You need a cool dip," she said. "Come on into the water. Look at these lovely shells I got – aren't they marvellous?"

"Marvellous," Greig said. "You look marvellous too. Now I've got used to it, that costume is very becoming."

"Becoming – what a funny way to describe it," Sarah laughed, but she was pleased at his commendation. "Come on, up you get."

She helped him to his feet, and then trotted down with him hand in hand to the water and had a sedate swim with him until more clanging from the region of the fire announced that tea had been made.

"What a marvellous idea!" Greig exclaimed when he saw what was on offer. "Exactly what I need to quench my thirst."

"I must say I wouldn't have thought of it," Sarah said,

following him up the beach," but I wouldn't say no."
The sun was past its meridian and the afternoon was cooler with long sloping shadows. Gulls were beginning to assemble on the beach just above the water line at the end farthest from the humans, and small red-legged sand birds ran in and out of the falling waves snapping up the lugworms that were exposed when the wave withdrew.

The party sat around sipping their tea with a quiet, almost somnolent air, and Sarah was reminded of children at the end of a long day out, worn out with excitement. Talk was desultory – everyone was pleasantly tired and content just to drowse and nod. Not long after that everyone had to collect up his belongings, and the whole party re-embarked for the journey back through the gathering dusk. The first stars were out before the sun had reached the horizon, and as the darkness crept over the sky, spirits began to revive in the coolness and people began to look forward to the dance that was to come.

"A nice refreshing shower when we get in," Greig said, "and a drink with lots of ice in it, and I shall feel fit for anything. I think that sleep did me good after all."

"More than you can say for some – look at the poor girl over there – she'll be sore tonight. How red she is!"

"You're very cheerful. Did you have a nice day while I was sleeping?"

"You didn't sleep all that long," Sarah countered. "But yes, I did have a nice day, on the whole. And I'm looking forward to this evening."

"So am I."

"I'm glad. I thought you'd flake out long before now.

What endurance," she laughed, and he squeezed her hand affectionately.

When they arrived back at the villa, they went straight to their 'cells' to shower and change for the evening. Sarah took the opportunity to wash her hair, which was thick with salt and sand, and rough-dried it with the small hand hairdryer she always took on holiday with her. Her hair was so long and thick she dared not leave it to chance to dry, or she'd have spent half her holiday in her room. The difference it made was amazing, and she was so relieved to have shed the sticky weight that had seemed attached to it that she spent some minutes running her hands through it to enjoy the silky feel. Shaken forward, it almost concealed the bruise on her cheek.

She chose a very thin, light dress of floral chiffon for the evening, which showed off plenty of her brown shoulders and upper bust. She kept her makeup simple, and wore no jewellery except – a last minute choice – her dolphin ring. Greig met her at the door to her room, and whistled softly.

"Lucky man who dances with *you* tonight," he said. "Madam, may I have the honour of escorting you to the dining room?"

"You may, sir," she said, and slipped her arm through his. He was so comfortable to be with when they were not quarrelling: it would be good to feel safe again, after tonight.

They had a drink in the bar, and then a leisurely meal of parma ham and salad followed by a water-ice flavoured with creme de menthe which just suited the hot evening, and then wandered out onto the verandah to watch the final preparations for the dance. An artificial floor was being laid for the serious dancers, both to give them a decent surface and to protect the already dying grass. The lights were lit amongst the trees, and the band was tuning up on their portable bandstand – it was a group of local youths, dressed in tight black trousers and slashed white shirts. The former disappeared against the background of the dark cypresses, and from a certain angle only the top half of them could be seen, playing disembodied.

"It's so lovely here," Sarah said contentedly. "Listen to those crickets! There must be millions of them."

Greig did not even correct her; he smiled at her rapturous face and stroked her hair back with a gentle hand and said, "Would you like to dance, or would you like another drink?"

"Both – but dance first," she said, and they stepped out onto the floor together.

When they had danced for a while, they relinquished their place to another couple, for dancing space was limited, and went back to the verandah and Sarah waited there, leaning her forearms on the cool stone balustrade while Greig went back inside to fetch drinks. There was evidently some hold-up at the bar, for he was gone rather a while, and while she was still waiting for him to come back, and strolling up and down the verandah, she saw Alec standing under the cypresses on the other side of the lawn.

A quick glance over her shoulder told her Greig was not in sight yet – this would be a good opportunity to get the business over with, and it wouldn't take a minute. She darted quickly across to where he was standing, looking in the opposite direction from her, but as she neared him he seemed to come to some decision, and slipped into the trees out of sight.

Bother, thought Sarah, and ran after him. She didn't want to call since she would rather not draw any attention to herself. The trees were only a thin belt on the cliff top and she was soon through to the other side, and saw Alec walking away from her along the cliff edge. She called him softly then, and he turned, saw her, and stood still until she could catch him up.

"Well?" he asked her, and there was no smile on his face.

"Well what?" she countered.

"I didn't think you'd come," he said, walking on without looking at her. She fell in beside him. "I saw you dancing. You looked – as though you were enjoying yourself."

"I was," Sarah said softly. "Weren't you?"

"Not any more," he said, and stopped again uncertainly. "I wondered – that is, I thought – " He paused again, and Sarah waited for him to make up his mind. She looked out over his shoulder at the sea, turned into a sheet of beaten silver by the brilliant moon and felt the soft air moving on her skin with no breath of coolness.

"What did you think?" she prompted quietly. He sighed and reached for his breast pocket.

"Never mind. We'd better get on with it. Here's the picture.

"Thanks," Sarah said, her fingers closing on it gladly, and she set her hand to tear it when Alec said,

"Aren't you going to look at it before you finish it off?"

She *hadn't* been going to, but she did when he spoke, turning it up to the moon to be able to see. There they were, locked in their apparent embrace, gazing into each other's eyes – the memory of it swept over her, the memory of his face so close to hers, the memory of the time he had kissed her. A feeling of weakness and confusion flooded her, and she looked up at him, her lips parted as if to ask a question, as if to seek enlightenment from him for what it was she felt.

His eyes glittered as he stepped closer to her, his long, mobile mouth was set firm. "Well, Sarah?" he said, and the way he spoke her name made her tremble. "Well, aren't you going to tear it up?" She could not drag her eyes away from his; they were held in a hypnotic gaze. "It was the bargain, remember."

Slowly she shook her head. "I can't," she said. "I don't want to. Here – " she held it out in a shaking hand. "You'd better have it back. I – "

"Sarah – " he said again. She was trembling from head to foot, her gaze fixed like a dazzled hare, but as he breathed her name for the third time she lifted her arms to him, and in a second he had closed his own about her and was crushing her lips with sweet, fierce kisses.

"Sarah, oh my darling Sarah," he whispered, kissing her mouth and her hot cheeks, her forehead, her silvery hair in a frenzy of emotion. He thrust both hands up into the silken mane and held her head still for more and still more kisses, and still she clung to him, dazed, but responding with a growing passion.

"I shouldn't – I mustn't – " she whispered, confused, and he drew back his head and looked at her penetratingly. The moonlight was in his face, and she wondered that she could ever have thought him merely funny, that she could ever have not noticed the beauty and strength of his face.

"I love you," he said, giving her a little shake as if to emphasise his words. "I've loved you since the first moment I saw you – and you love me too. You do, don't you, Sarah?"

"I don't know – I – yes, yes I do," she said at last, and though he had seemed so sure, he enveloped her in a close embrace and murmured,

"Thank God!" He was silent for a moment, and then said, "When I saw you tonight with him, dancing, and looking so happy, I thought I had been mistaken after all. I was walking about all evening wondering what to do, wondering how you really felt. Then when you came after me – I hoped, but I still wasn't sure."

"What do you mean – you weren't sure? Why did you think – ?"

"I knew from the beginning that you weren't in love with him, that you had drifted into a mere habit with him. But I knew that you didn't know your own heart, and I hoped to show it to you. But you were stubborn – " and now, for the first time, he smiled, that familiar, curling smile, half mocking, half tender. Sarah, however, had other things on her mind.

"Greig," she said. "What can I say to him? How can I explain?"

"You're worried?"

"He was always so jealous. The last thing in the world I want to do is hurt him – "

"I wasn't going to say this," Alec said. "I was going to let you do things your own way, but after all – " He hesitated, then, "While I was watching you, I was watching him too. There were one or two moments – I don't think you'll find him too hard to explain to."

"I don't understand," Sarah said.

"I'll say no more," Alec said. "But one thing is sure – you must tell him tonight – you mustn't go on any longer with what your heart isn't in."

"You're right, of course," Sarah said. "But he's so dear to me – I don't want ever to hurt him. He'll be looking for me now, I've no doubt."

"You'd better go. Be brave. Kiss me once more, and then – "

Again she turned her face up to him for the solace, the heady delight of his mouth on hers, and when at last she would tear herself away he held her close, her head on his shoulder, his face against her hair.

"I could stay here with you for ever," he said softly. "I don't want ever to let you go."

And a moment later she was running back through the dark shadow of the cypresses towards the lights and noise of the villa.

The encounter on the cliff seemed to Sarah to have lasted half the night, but it could not have been more than a couple of minutes, for when she came out onto the lawn she saw Greig standing on the verandah looking about for her, with a glass in each hand. She hurried across to him.

181

"Ah, there you are," he said, handing her her glass. "I wondered where you were." He said it, however, without seeming to want an answer, for which Sarah was grateful. He looked at her kindly but rather absently, and then said in a voice that she could have sworn, if she didn't know Greig so well, was embarrassed, "Let's find somewhere quiet to sit down. I want to talk to you."

Shaking a little with trepidation she followed him as he led the way round the side of the villa and through the small side passage that led into the grassy square outside their 'cells'. The noise of the dance was distant and muted here, and in the sudden quiet they could hear the fountain tinkling into its bowl like a sylvan music of its own.

"We'll sit on the fountain's edge," Greig said, leading the way. The bowl of the fountain had a wide, comfortable rim, on which they could stand their glasses as well as sit. The grass court was half in shadow, which made the lawn look black and cold, but the fountain was caught in the strong, eery moonlight, and the flickering, tumbling waters shone like quicksilver.

"What did you want to talk to me about?" Sarah asked him, forcing herself to be calm.

"Sarah," he began, "you know I'm very fond of you, don't you?"

"Yes, I do," she said. "You asked me that once before, don't you remember?"

"I do," he said. "Several times I've been on the verge of saying this – but I wasn't sure." He paused thoughtfully. "Well, I have to speak now, now I've keyed myself up. Sarah, I've wondered once or twice recently, if perhaps your feelings have changed towards me?" Sarah could not have answered at once, and it was as well that he hurried on without waiting for an answer,

"We've been together now for a long time, and from the beginning everyone has been telling us that we're two opposites. I suppose that's why we were attracted to each other in the beginning, because we were so very different, and it's a pretty good rule of thumb – but first attraction isn't the same as a lasting relationship."

He looked at her to see if she understood him, and went on again, "As a rule, I think it's better for like people to marry rather than unalike. And I've wondered quite a lot recently if we would be happy together if we were to get married. You see, you're such a lively, outgoing person, always eager for excitement and fun and noise, and I'm a dull, quiet kind of person, who loves nothing better than to stay at home with a good book. I wonder if being married to me might not be too dull for you."

It was necessary to speak then, but all she could say was, "I don't know what to say."

Greig seemed relieved that she had not burst into tears or flown at him in a rage. "I've been watching you, especially since we came on holiday, and I wouldn't have mentioned it if I hadn't thought that perhaps you were feeling much as I was. I'm still willing to give it a try if you want, because I'm very fond of you – very, very fond – " He stopped, and then gave a shaky grin. "Say something, Sarah, even if it's 'go to hell'."

"Greig, I'm – I hardly know how to begin." She collected her thoughts and said, "I was going to speak to you on the same subject tonight, but you've forestalled me." Greig looked surprised and, she was afraid, hurt, and she reached out for his hands without even knowing it. "I'm very fond of you, too. You're my dearest friend, the closest friend I've ever had – but you're right. My feelings have changed. I don't feel in love with you any more. In fact," gathering her courage, "I know I'm not in love with you. Don't be hurt – I can't help it."

"It would be illogical to be hurt, when I've just told you the same thing, wouldn't it?" he said, trying to smile.

"Yes, very illogical, but all the same very understandable. I feel a bit that way too. But you're right. We wouldn't be happy married – we're too different, we'd quarrel all the time and make each other miserable. I'd always be disturbing you when you wanted to work or study, and I'd be too frivolous to entertain your important clients and so on."

She stopped and there was a silence between them, filled with the silvery sound of the fountain, and suddenly, from somewhere close, the liquid notes of a nightingale. Listening, Sarah found tears very close to the surface.

"What do we do?" she whispered. Greig squeezed her hand comfortingly.

"We can still be friends. I'll still be here to tell your troubles to and get you out of scrapes – although – "

"Yes?"

"Not all your scrapes. But perhaps there's someone else you turn to for those?"

"You know?" she said softly.

"I wondered. I saw him look at you once or twice. I didn't know if you felt the same way."

184

"I don't quite know how I feel," Sarah said honestly. "I want to find out. But, Greig – you know I never meant to hurt or do badly by you?"

"Yes, I know. We can part friends." He added softly to himself, "It was him, then."

"What?"

"I felt it, that day we were all three together. I felt somehow that it was you and him, and that I was the outsider. But it was a good day after all," he added, sounding almost surprised at the realisation. "We can still be friends – all three."

"And you? What about you?" Sarah asked anxiously. The nightingale sang again, and they stopped to listen. Greig looked down at her and smiled kindly.

"Don't worry about me. I've got my exams to keep me occupied."

"Oh Greig – "

"Hush, infant, I'm teasing. Don't worry – I mean it. We've both got a lot of living ahead of us. Nothing much has changed."

"I hope you find someone soon," she said.

"I expect I will," Greig replied easily. "Well now, we'd better get back to the party. We've still got another week of our holiday left – anything might happen."

"Yes," Sarah said more brightly, "and there are some very nice girls here." Greig laughed.

"That's my girl! Keep the chin up. Now just kiss me one last time, and then you'd better go and find him – is he waiting for you somewhere?"

"I think so – on the cliff top."

"I don't think he'll be too much surprised at what we've

been saying. I've an idea he knows which way the wind blows."

"He said the same about you," Sarah said. "It strikes me I've been the only one around here blind deaf and dumb to everything."

They stood up, and Greig bent his head to give her one last, chaste kiss on the lips, and they walked back out through the passage and parted on the edge of the lawn. Her heart singing with gladness, Sarah ran, threading her way through the crowds; glad that Greig was not unhappy, glad that the confusion of the last few days was cleared away for ever. She understood so much now – all his odd moods and questioning looks, everything that had seemed unaccountable. She ran through the dark fringe of trees and out into the moonlight of the cliff where Alec was waiting for her, pacing anxiously up and down, waiting for her to end his doubts.

As soon as he saw her, he knew everything that had happened, and they ran towards each other to meet in a glad embrace.

"It's all right," she said, and winding their arms about each other they walked on beside the moonlit, timeless sea, held wrapt in the silence of an enchanted place.